Also by

Kristine Kathryn Rusch

She didn't know how, but he'd found her...

STEFFIE SHOVED HER hands in the pocket of her tweed pants, then headed down the asphalt walk. The strange man hurried behind her, his feet scuffling.

"You know," he said softly, his torso brushing hers, his legs keeping pace with her legs, "there's a ten million credit reward for anyone who identifies you."

"Ten million?" she asked, a bit startled at the amount. Last she had heard it was two million. "That low?"

He laughed, not fooled. "You're hot, girl, and some cools want to find you."

He spoke softly as he walked with her, his words like a caress in her ear. She didn't know how he found her, didn't know who he worked for, didn't know what he wanted.

The not knowing terrified her.

But she didn't show it. She didn't allow anything to show on her face.

"Such a strange creature you make me out to be," she said.

"They don't call you Steffie Storm-Warning for nothing." He had her name.

COOLHUNTING

KRISTINE KATHRYN RUSCH

Coolhunting

Copyright © 2018 Kristine Kathryn Rusch
First published in Science Fiction Age, July, 1998.
Published by WMG Publishing
Cover and Layout copyright © 2018 by WMG Publishing
Cover art copyright © 2018 Philcold/Dreamstime
ISBN-13: 978-1-56146-644-3
ISBN-10: 1-56146-644-1

COOLHUNTING

FIFTEEN DIFFERENT WAYS to fasten a shoelace and she was sitting on the porch steps of a refurbished brownstone, watching a boy barely old enough to shave tie knots in an ancient pair of Air Jordans. Steffie pushed her hair out of her face, opened her palmtop and used the tiny lens in the corner to shoot the boy's hands. They were long, slender, unlined, with wide knuckles and trimmed nails. A person couldn't do what he was doing with short stubby fingers or InstaGrow™ nails that curved like talons.

He took all six multi-colored laces, wrapped them around three fingers, and created bows of differing sizes. Then he tied them at the tongue, and created a flower that blossomed from the ancient shoe like a rose in the middle of rubble.

When he was done, she flipped him a plastic. He caught it between his thumb and forefinger, glanced at it, and raised his eyebrows.

"Mega," he said.

She was glad he thought so. She only paid him half the going rate for a style that would be all over the streets in the next two hours, then all over the stores in the next two weeks.

"Thanks," she said, and slipped her palmtop back in her pocket.

Then she grabbed one of his extra laces, tied her brown hair back, and headed down the gum-covered sidewalk toward the park.

Shoelaces. Who'd have thought? When shoes could zip, velcro, and seal themselves, who'd've thought the arbiters of cool would go back to the lace?

Hers was not to ask why. Hers was to record, market, and change.

Coolhunting was still a strange profession, but thirty years after the first coolhunters hit the streets, it had worked its way into a mini-science.

A science only a person with an eye for beauty and a sense of people could spot.

She resisted the urge to open her palmtop and check her own credit account. She'd sent the vid to seven laces companies, two shoe manufacturers, and one hundred resale outlets. Each of them should have sent a fee into her current account. It should have doubled with the laces bit. If she hit her quota today, she'd have enough for a two-week flop.

Lord knew she needed it. Her own boots were worn thin from all the walking. Twenty-one successful hunts in seven days, not to mention eight busts, and one illegal.

She still held the record for the most shifts in one day. Steffie Storm-Warning, they called her, because in her wake was turmoil and destruction. Entire companies folded on the basis of her vids. Entire companies replaced them. And credits flowed back and forth like a river covered in Mediterranean sludge.

No one knew who she was. She had forty different legal identities, and more than enough credits stashed in various accounts to live expensively for the rest of her life. But she liked coolhunting. It was purposely anonymous—if people knew who she was, they would chase her, try to convince her they were cool—and it carried no responsibility. She didn't answer to a boss, she didn't answer to a company, she didn't even answer to the people she sold her vids to. She was as independent as independent got, a loner in every sense of the word.

And she liked it like that.

On the corner a hot dog vender floated his cart over a hot air grate. The dogs weren't like the ones she'd had as a kid. These were all meat, registered and certified lean cuts from prime portions of pig. The taste was similar but not the same.

A taste gone from her life.

Everything changed.

Nothing remained the same.

Life on the street had taught her that.

Coolhunting had reinforced it.

She took an unmarked plastic from her pocket, checked the credit level, and decided to launder it through the vendor. She stopped, ordered two dogs slathered in mustard, sweet catsup, and pickle relish, and handed the man the plastic.

He was skinny, unshaven, with an apron that had

grime on it as old as she was. Vendors had always looked like that. Even in the ancient black 'n white vids available for free download on any TV set, the vendors looked like that.

A hundred years hadn't changed them. Just their carts and their product.

He took her plastic, ran it through his machine, then frowned. "That's a lot of change," he said.

"Just run it through the machine." She took one dog off his countertop, and took a bite. A little too juicy, a little too ham-flavored, but enough to still an appetite that had been building for the good part of a day.

"Don't do that any more," he said. Anyone caught recharging too much plastic, running too many credits, was brought in.

"Sure you do, for an extra five," she said around the dog.

He grunted, then slammed the plastic into his machine. No one said no to an extra five, and she could afford it. She could afford anything if she were willing to spend credits instead of accumulate them.

Somehow, knowing how fast tastes changed, made her unwilling to commit to her own.

She ate the rest of the dog, nearly swallowing the last piece whole. Maybe it had been two days since she'd eaten. Maybe only a few hours. She couldn't remember. She'd been hunting.

It always took all of her energy.

As she picked up the second dog, he handed the plastic back to her.

"I won't do it again," he said.

"Your loss." She sprayed a bit of bun at him, and automatically covered her mouth with her left hand. "Sorry."

He shrugged, turned away. A lot of basically honest people did that when she asked them to violate their own rules. Made her ashamed sometimes. Made her realize how different her world was from theirs.

She had the luxury of eating the second dog more slowly, then cleaning her mustard-covered hands and face in the stand's laser wipe. She grabbed a napkin and wiped for good measure: public cleaners always left her feeling a bit gritty.

"Good dogs?"

She hadn't seen the guy approach. She glanced up as he spoke, registered him as someone she'd seen before, and a shudder ran down her back. He wasn't young like most of her subjects, but then her early subjects weren't young any more either. Still, his clear gray eyes slanting in a coffee-colored Slavic-feature face looked familiar.

The wrong kind of familiar.

She shrugged, kept it light. "Dogs are as good as any these days."

"You ever had the old ones?" He brushed a hand over his silver suit. Three weeks old, worn Detroit style, with a red cummerbund instead of a tie and pierce chain. "The ones they made of sawdust and pig's feet?"

"That's not how they made 'em," she said and stepped away from him.

For a minute, she thought he'd keep up, but he didn't. He stayed at the stand, bought himself a dog, and watched her walk away.

Maybe that was how her subjects felt when she

watched them. As if they were suddenly on public display, as if their entire selves were being exposed to the world.

Watchers shouldn't be watched.

She rounded a corner, then slipped into the park.

The air was fresher here, the trees budding. Tulips bloomed in special garden circles maintained by a crew of city employees who were determined to make Central Park look as cultivated as possible. She liked to spend spring here. It made her feel alive.

It also allowed her to watch the cools bloom.

She went to her bench. It was newly painted—green this time—to give the illusion of newness despite its great age. Around her, couples threw balls for their dogs, and kids went by in groups, deep in conversation.

She watched:

Clothes.

Shoes.

Jewelry.

Always alert for a new combination, a new look. But it wasn't as easy as all that. The look was a sense, a third eye, a way of seeing that most people didn't have.

She wasn't looking so much for the new trend as she was for the person who would set that trend.

Back when coolhunting started in hype-filled '90s, the coolhunter's goal was to find the cool kid, the one who would be the innovator, the one all the other kids wanted to copy. But what the early coolhunters never realized was that cool itself was a transient state: a cool kid one week would be passé the next.

Cool was easy to spot.

Pre-cool was hard.

And she had the hardest job of all. She was in New York, not Phoenix or Dallas or Santa Fe, those hotbeds of the newest trends. Here she had to work harder because everyone knew that fashion moved north and east. It started in the southwest and traveled, slowly through the south, up the middle, then over to the eastern seaboard.

Coolhunting in New York was like deep-sea diving in the Arctic: Not recommended.

Which made it all the more challenging.

Which meant it was for her.

She settled onto the iron bench. It was still a bit cold to be sitting still, but she had two dogs to settle and that encounter to put in place. Strangers rarely spoke to her. She put up an invisible barrier: if she was noticed it was in passing. If she wasn't, even better.

Casual people didn't speak to her on the street.

This guy knew her.

And if he knew her, he'd be here, sometime soon.

In the meantime, she'd hunt.

THE NICE THING about New York in the spring was that everyone came to her. After the winter cooped up in high heat flats, ThermalTemp All-Weather Gear™, and Footsnugger Boots™, the city's residents wanted to strut their stuff. Cool happened fast here in the spring: trends among the setters ran hourly. The early adapters spent only days in the new styles before moving onto something else. Even the herd, the followers, only spent a few weeks in the style before changing, and the laggers never caught the spring rush.

Last spring, she'd cleared 30 million credits in one month.

This spring, she hoped to do better.

She leaned back on the bench, feeling its chill permeate her '01 vintage sweater. Her stomach churned restlessly, disturbed by too much food and that stranger's face.

Teenagers walked in front of her, laughing, the girls with their hair short and spiky, the boys with theirs down to their knees. Two-year-old fashions: these were laggers who really didn't care about their position. They were not the architects of cool that she wanted.

Sometimes, though, sometimes she envied them their easy walk, their uncaring laughter. Her life had become so focused on trends and styles, on the way that clothing—appearance—reflected thought that she wondered if she ever made decisions all on her own any more. She wouldn't think of wearing spiky hair, nor would she walk in a crowd, laughing.

She missed the laughter.

Coolhunting made close companionship impossible. Friendships difficult. More and more lately she'd been thinking of retiring, of finding a flat in the city and actually having contact with people.

Making friends.

Establishing ties.

A boy, no more than ten, air-shoed past, running six inches off the ground. His shoes, early models, formed a cushion of air that was as dangerous as it was once thought safe: the air cushion acted like a super high platform. One false step and the wearer would fall.

To run in air-shoes required guts and a certain amount of I-don't-care.

She almost got up and followed him. Almost.

His spirit was unique, but she saw nothing that could be duplicated. Nothing that she could vid and sell. Air-shoes had been on the market since the teens, and had had their moment six months ago when the nets declared them unsafe.

Still, she had never seen anyone run in them before.

"I'd've thought you'd have followed him." The man from the hot-dog stand sat next to her. He smelled faintly of spicy cologne, and he had a touch of mustard on the corner of his mouth. It made him seem more real, somehow.

"Why would I follow him?" she asked, then wished she hadn't. She knew better than to engage.

"I'd've picked him," the man said, "if I were cool-hunting."

"Which you're not," she said.

"Who says?" He touched the shoelace in her hair.

She stood. "I do."

Her hands were shaking. She shoved them in the pocket of her tweed pants, then headed down the asphalt walk. He hurried behind her, his feet scuffling. She could smell him before he reached her.

That cologne was beginning to annoy.

"You know," he said softly, his torso brushing hers, his legs keep pacing with her legs, "there's a ten million credit reward for anyone who identifies you."

"Ten million?" she asked, a bit startled at the amount. Last she had heard it was two million. "That low?"

He laughed, not fooled. "You're hot, girl, and some cools want to find you."

He spoke softly as he walked with her, his words like a caress in her ear. She didn't know how he found her, didn't know who he worked for, didn't know what he wanted.

The not knowing terrified her.

But she didn't show it. She didn't allow anything to show on her face.

"Such a strange creature you make me out to be," she said.

"They don't call you Steffie Storm-Warning for nothing."

He had her name. Other corporate headhunters had found her before—a coolhunter always revealed herself in the moment of payment—but none of them had known who she was.

They had been dumb and obvious and she'd been able to give them the slip.

She couldn't slip him. He was still pressed against her, as if they were lovers on a midday stroll.

She kept walking, but her breath was coming shallowly now. She hoped he didn't notice.

"You know," she snapped, "there are about eighteen laws you're breaking touching me like that."

"You want to go to the cops?" he asked and she could hear the smile in his voice.

"No," she said. "I want you to back off."

She stopped suddenly and he slammed into her, nearly losing his balance. She shoved with her elbow, and he fell hard enough on the grass to let out a small grunt.

A girl stopped beside her and peered down. "He all right?" the girl asked. She was wired. Small chips dotted her face like jewelry. In the quick glance that Steffie got, she recognized audio, video, and net chips.

"He doesn't need to be," Steffie said.

"Ooo," the girl said. "Want me to get someone?" She tapped a chip on her chin. Security system too. The girl had money.

"Naw," Steffie said. "I think he got the idea."

The girl laughed and continued, but not before Steffie

caught a glimpse of her shoes. Scuffed Air Jordans with six laces tied in a flower bow.

An early adapter.

The vid had already hit the street.

The man was sitting up, a hand to his head. Steffie pushed him back down and put a foot on his chest. She got the distinct sense he was humoring her, that he could shove her aside with a flick of the wrist.

She didn't care. It was the look that counted. And right now it looked as if she were in control.

"I don't know who you are or what you want," she said. "But leave me alone."

"Can't do that." He put a hand on her boot. "Italian leather. Nice. They don't make stuff this soft anymore."

She yanked her foot away. "What do you want?" she asked.

"Well, I don't want to broadcast your id," he said. "If I wanted that, I could have done it by now."

He was right. He had obviously seen her long before she saw him. The thought made her even more uneasy.

"You're one of those stalkers, aren't you?" she asked, yanking her foot away. "Interested in the hunt, in toying with your prey, in killing slowly."

He smiled as he sat up, and rubbed the grass stains out of his sleeve. "You have a vivid imagination."

"I want to know why you're bothering me," she said. *And how you know who I am.* But she didn't say that. She had already said too much.

"It's not enough to say that I'm an admirer?"

"No," she said.

"Well, I am."

"Then admire from a distance."

"And let you dive away like you did before, only to come back with a new look, a new style."

"Maybe I'll retire," she said.

"Maybe," he said. "But you haven't yet. And you have more than enough to live on. You don't need to be on the streets, but they're in your blood."

She was so thoroughly chilled now that gooseflesh had risen on her arms. No one knew this much about her. No one. She had made certain there wasn't much information about her anywhere. Sometimes she wasn't sure she had that much information about herself.

"What do you want?" she asked for the third and final time.

He spread out his hands. They were empty. "Let me up?" he asked.

She took her foot off his chest. He stood, brushed himself off, and adjusted the silver jacket. His cummerbund had twisted so that the self-sealing seam showed.

This time he kept his distance, and eyed her warily.

"Fashions have come and gone in the time it's taking you to answer this question," she said.

He wiped the mustard stain from the side of his mouth, glanced at his fingertips, winced and rubbed them together as if he could make the mustard go away.

"Your family sent me," he said.

She went hot, then cold, then hot again. She hadn't thought of her family in years.

Not true.

She thought of them every day.

She hadn't spoken to them in years.

"Really?" she asked, with the right amount of sarcasm.

His smile was patient. "I didn't expect you to believe me," he said. "And neither did they. They set up a home site accessible only to you, with names and numbers you'd know, they said. And the only way you can locate it is with this chip."

He held out his palm. In it was a red chip case the size of a sequin.

She stared at it. "For all I know that could scramble my system or blow me away."

He didn't move. "They told me to tell you that KD is dying."

Those hot/cold flashes ran through her again. "KD?" she said before she could stop herself. "That's not possible."

"That's what they said."

She squinted, unsure whether to trust, unsure whether to try. "And you are?" she asked.

"Unimportant," he said and flipped the chip case toward her.

She caught it in her left hand as he disappeared into the park.

SHE PUT THE chip in the special nip pouch she'd had carved below her belly button. Nip pouches were expensive, because they were for the criminal or paranoid. Hers was big enough to hold a wrist-top and the surgeon had been good enough so that the pouch's opening looked like part of her belly button itself.

Then she went back to work.

—Caught a middle-aged woman topless, showing off surgically enhanced breasts. Micropoodles—dyed pink and gold—were leashed to her nipple chains. Steffie hated it, but knew it would catch on with the fifty and older crowd, the aging Gen Xers who loved to torture their already burdened flesh.

(The chip lay cold against her skin, irritating, like a grain of sand in her eye.)

—Found a young man playing guitar beside a fountain, who looked as if he'd been dipped in gold. Gold hair, gold skin, gold eyes. As the light shifted, his colors deepened.

She filmed a while, catching his transition from gold to bronze, bronze to brown. She didn't know what he used, and didn't ask when she flipped him his plastic. Someone would know, and someone would pay, several someones, depending on how she put it across the nets.

(The chip tingled, as if it were a live thing. Reminding her...)

—Had the palmtop out, already filming an androgen's roped fingernails when she saw the identical twins, captured in miniature, holding their keeper's hand. They strolled through the park wearing frilly white, their eyes old and bored and—

She shut the vid off, slid her hand across her belly, and pressed the chip.

KD's dying.

She shoved the palmtop in her pocket, and headed out of the park.

To Leo's.

LEO WORKED OUT of his apartment in a rundown condominium complex at the cross of Riverside and West 94th. The building dated from the 1980s when it was posh. A lot of the original owners still lived in the buildings, but children and grandchildren who inherited had no respect for history. Leo was one of those. He liked the space and the old charm, but he hated the snobbishness that went with it.

Hence the little dive shop he ran out of his first floor apartment's kitchen.

She used the code he'd given her five years before to subvert the security system. It too was once state-of-the-art, in the post-doorman, high tech days, but even with updates, a street kid could get in with a few security chips and a beeper. Most of the residents wore their own security these days and didn't care, but a handful of the elderly ones had no idea how people like Leo compromised their safety.

People like Leo, and people like Steffie.

She knew a few electronic tricks of her own, and had used them often enough to gain a flop in a high security building. She never took anything except a little space and a little privacy, and she was sure the residents never noticed.

They always had space and privacy to spare.

Leo kept his door unlocked. After her fifth visit to him, she realized he didn't live in the apartment, only worked there, and didn't really care about the credits he made. Someone could—and often did—rip him off, and he continued, as if nothing had changed. She finally realized he was like her. The credits didn't matter; the challenge did.

She slid through the oak door and ran a hand over the motion detector that controlled the lights.

"Leo?"

"Kitchen, babe," he said, voice floating past the vintage mid-twentieth century furniture. His tastes ran to chrome and plastic, stuff once considered cheap by the very people who initially lived in this building. Not cheap any longer. His couch, with its chrome legs that swooped into uncomfortable arms, and orange plastic seat, ran in the range of several thousand credits.

She slipped through the remodeled arch doorway into his dark and dingy kitchen. It smelled of oranges. Peels littered the floor. Her boots made small sucking sounds as she walked.

Leo hunched over the oak table he'd inherited with the apartment, using a welding tool as old as his couch to solder some metal together. She watched him work, seeing the small shield before his face shimmer in the old fashioned light.

Then he shut off the torch, turned and the shield faded to nothing.

He grinned. "Been a while, babe."

She knew his name, but he didn't know hers. She liked it that way; he didn't mind. She suspected he wasn't named Leo at all, suspected it was as much an affectation as the rest of the place.

She shrugged. "Been busy."

With a wave of a hand, he raised the lights. They didn't cut the gloom, but they illuminated his face and hers. His was mid-forties, careworn, no enhancements or lines. His eyes were a faded blue, his lips painted a pale maroon.

"Whatcha got?"

She was clutching the chip in her hand, and had been since she left the park. He didn't need to know about the nip pouch.

She came closer and opened her fist. The chip case gleamed in the odd light. "A man gave this to me. Said it was important."

"And you took it?" Leo raised a scarred eyebrow. He leaned over her palm, stared at the case, then reached behind himself and grabbed a tweezers. He picked the case up using the tweezers and set it on a clear sheet of glass.

"You should know better than to touch something like this, babe," Leo said.

"I do," she said.

"But he gotcha, right? What'd he do, tell you it's full of credits?"

"No," she said, unwilling to say anymore.

Leo shook his head. "I'll check it out for you. Want me to siphon the information off it?"

"Tell me what's there first," she said, "and if it's booby-trapped."

He grinned. "You give me all the fun jobs."

She shrugged. She'd never given him a job like this before.

"Head into the main room, wouldja? And can you wait? This might take some time."

"I can wait," she said, and left the kitchen.

The main room of his apartment overlooked Riverside, but the windows were so streaked with grime, she could barely see through them. His vid equipment was old and obviously for client use.

She sat on the couch, put her hand in her hair, and found the shoelace. She yanked it out, let her hair fall into her face, and wrapped the lace around her fingers. It was worn and old, fraying on the sides. Like the laces of the first pair of tennis shoes she'd had when she was a child.

KD had loved those shoes.

Big people shoes, she had said, wistfully.

"Big people shoes," Steffie murmured. She didn't want to think about KD. She leaned back, put an arm over her eyes, and let herself drift. This was as good a place to flop as any. Besides, she needed the rest.

[5]

IT WAS DARK when Leo woke her. He was wearing a personal light on each shoulder. They illuminated his face and a small circular area around him. The couch, the stained wood floor, and part of a ripped rug stood out in sharp relief.

He was holding the chip case between his thumb and forefinger—a good sign.

"It performs an instant download from a prearranged site," he said. "It forces the computer it's in to go to that site, and remain there until the download's complete. Theoretically, the site is rigged so that only the people who can answer certain questions can get it, but I circumvented it. The site's computer is in Nebraska. It links to a system in Kansas City, then links to another system in Austin. All checked out clean. No traps. And no real traps built into this thing except the instant download."

"Which someone could trace to my system."

"In a nanosecond," he said. His grin increased. "But not to mine."

She took the chip from him. "You got something like that for me?"

"I thought you'd never ask," he said. Then his smile disappeared. "Although I don't know why you'd want to. The site is your basic family crap. Genealogies, old photographs, histories, loss of former holdings, that sort of thing."

She rubbed the sleep off her face, hoping to keep any fleeting expression from him. "That's okay," she said.

"Your family?" he asked.

"I doubt it," she said. "Just some weirdness with my work."

"You sure, babe?" and this time his voice held concern. "I wouldn't want to give you something that'll get you in trouble. Of any kind."

"You found more trouble on there?"

He shook his head. "But folks don't normally bring this kinda stuff to me, you know? They bring me—" he paused, as if considering his words "—well, you know, stuff I would expect. Illegals, traps, listings no one should see. Not something this tame."

"And that scares you?" she asked.

"Different. Anything different. It's not good, you know."

She smiled. "Actually," she said. "I thrive on different."

[6]

THE EQUIPMENT WEIGHED her down. She was
used to a palmtop, some plastic and nothing more. Leo gave
her a laptop the size of a purse and told her to dump it
when she was done.

She took an aircab to Chinatown, found a basement
restaurant where no one seemed to speak English, and took
a booth in the back. The decor was as old as the stuff in
Leo's apartment. If it weren't for the singletops for sale at
the front desk, the tiny access ports built into the centers of
the tables, and the program-it-yourself wall displays beside
each booth she'd have thought she'd entered some old flat
black-and-white.

The lighting was dim, the booth ripped, and the soy
sauce bottle so old that the red words were scraped off the
glass. She ordered by pointing to three numbers on the wall
display instead of talking to a waitress as she usually would
have done. She liked having the opportunity to practice her
Mandarin. It wasn't one of the recommended languages.

She was fluent in eight non-recommended, and all seven recommended. It made the hunt easier, being able to speak the language of the people she came across.

There wasn't much hunting here. She checked it out the moment she sat down. An elderly woman wore a red silk dress that looked like it belonged at a pre-turn luau. Two business women came in sporting cats-eye glasses that had been in fashion on Wednesday three weeks before. A middle-aged man had staked out a table, and was eating slowly from six different plates. He wore the big jeans and oversized shirt that had been in style when he was a boy. She called people like that the fashion careless.

She didn't need to work. She'd had a profitable day despite the interruptions. She could continue to hunt, or she could see what this chip was all about.

She set the laptop on the table, and plugged the chip into the slot Leo had showed her. Instantly the 'top booted up, logged on, and started a download. She took a sip of tea and watched as her family history scrolled across the screen. A waitress set down a plate of egg rolls, and Steffie grabbed one, even though her stomach was churning.

Fifteen generations of history, then her own face flashed across the screen, aged ten, the last known formal full family portrait. Steffie didn't need to look. She already knew the image: Parents in the back, her father's crewcut looking dated even now, her mother's nose ring catching the light. Grandparents behind them, looking staid, her paternal grandfather's long hair a mass of gray curls. Five children, various ages, Steffie the apparent oldest, with the baby Lana cuddled in her mother's arms. Her twin brothers flanking Steffie, and of course, KD.

KD.

She sat on Steffie's lap, wearing a ruffled white dress and patent leather shoes that had belonged to their great-grandmother Svetlana. Her unnaturally blonde hair was combed in ringlets, and her rosy cheeks blended into skin that past generations had once described as porcelain.

But her eyes. Her eyes belied it all.

Hooded and rebellious, they caught and reflected all the anger that no one else in the shot expressed. Steffie remembered holding the tiny body, remembered its tension, remembered how the anger molded each underdeveloped muscle.

KD is dying.

That's not possible.

But it was. Only not yet. Not for another three, maybe four decades.

Impossible.

A ploy to get her to contact the family?

Maybe.

But there were better ones.

Only her parents had never thought of them.

[7]

IT TOOK HER a while to find the message embedded in the coding. They used the standard questions, the ones everyone answered easily—birthdate, along with city, state, and county code. Taxpayer identification number, resident identification number, and working resident identification number. Following that was a retinal scan (she wondered how Leo had gotten around that one) and a left thumbprint match.

Most of the questions she subverted as well. She hadn't typed her personal numbers in nearly fifteen years. She couldn't remember her resident number, and she didn't have a working resident number. Even if she did, she wouldn't have given it up. She liked her privacy, and required it for the most part so that she could do her job. Her on-line identities were multiple and clear to her: her real one was lost in the haze of memory.

When she found the hidden message, the machine gave

her an instant hardcopy. She wondered if it had done that for Leo, as well. Only he wouldn't have understood the message.

KD dying. Wants to see you. Come back. You don't have to talk to us. But see her this one last time.

We hired several detectives and a bounty hunter. The detectives couldn't locate you. The hunter did but would not give your location. He did, however, volunteer to deliver this chip.

We would have included a pre-paid ticket on a same hour shuttle, but we don't know your city of origin. We are still willing to pay your way home.

Nothing has changed here. You know where to find us.

There was no signature. There didn't need to be. She recognized her father's abrupt tones in the words. Amazing how deep those memories went, how deep the effect of the lives that first touched hers. She hadn't spoken to her father in years, and yet she could still hear his voice in her mind, feel his presence as clearly as if she had left him yesterday.

She logged off, closed the laptop and ripped up the hardcopy, stuffing the pieces into her nip pouch for later disposal. Then she closed her eyes and leaned her head back, wishing her life could be as simple as it had been only ten hours ago.

"Are you all right?" the waitress asked in Mandarin.

"Fine," Steffie replied in the same language. Then she sipped the rest of her tea, paid with unmarked plastic, grabbed the laptop, and left.

[8]

SHE TOOK THE first shuttle she could grab. It departed from the rooftop pad at 63rd and Lex an hour after she left the restaurant. It had taken her nearly as long to get to the pad as it would take her to get to Ann Arbor.

It had been ten years since she'd been outside of Manhattan. Ten years since she'd arrived, fresh from Austin, then the cool-hunting capitol of the country. She'd arrived with a few credentials and a lot of balls, ready to take the plunge that most hunters fail:

Staking out her own hunting grounds, making her place the secret center of cool.

Austin lost its spot because everyone knew that cool-ness originated there. So early adapters arrived, followed by the trend-followers, and the cool-wanna-bes. Inundated by copycats, hunters, and wanna-bes, the truly cool left, and it took hunters almost a year to find the next center.

Phoenix.

Only no one advertised it.

Steffie didn't want to follow the cool ones. She wanted to find them. So she had come here, figuring that many of the cool were among the poor and unable to afford same-hour shuttles or even day transport. Every city in America, she figured, maybe even every city in the world had cool. She only had to find it.

And she knew none of the other hunters would come here, the heartland of American misery, the decaying edge of the known universe, where trends had not been set, really set, since the early part of the last century.

No one could come here.

Except her.

The shuttle was sleek and small. It sat on the rooftop like a black bird, wings permanently outstretched. A pilot sat up front and three other passengers were stepping into the back.

She punched her ticket code into the monitor, and watched as the electronic security shield shimmered into nothingness. She stepped across and heard a hum as it started up again.

As she climbed into the shuttle, she saw only ten passenger seats, and only five were full. Not much cause to go to Michigan in the late evening. She sank into the leather chair, fastened her belt and closed her eyes.

It would take five minutes from take-off to landing. Barely enough time to rest her eyes. Certainly not enough time to rethink the trip.

The shuttle landed on a concrete quad behind brick dorms on the University of Michigan campus. Steffie was the first to exit. She crossed the quad and entered the security gate, using one of her alias's codes to get through the scanning equipment.

She stopped when she made it outside. Snow still covered the ground although the sidewalks were bare. The air was cool and dry, and had a familiar smell, one she couldn't identify as anything more than childhood, than Ann Arbor.

Than home.

At the last word, she winced. She hadn't had a home for fifteen years, and she had liked it like that. Coolhunting suited her, with its insistence on anonymity, the constant need to keep trolling, the lack of attachments.

But here, here she was Stephanie Wyton-Brew, the second daughter of Andrew Wyton and Jennifer Brew, granddaughter of Elmer and Elise Wyton and Anthony and Josephine Brew.

And sister of KD.

She squared her shoulders, hoping they were strong enough to handle all that weight of the past, of an identity long lost. The house was just past the university, up on a hilly avenue whose name was lost in the fogs of her memory, near trees so old their canopied tops shrouded streets that had been built wide enough for carriages.

She had forgotten the name, but she hadn't forgotten how to get there. The way to the house she had grown up in was embedded as deeply into her memory as her father's voice.

Her stomach churned. She had nothing to say to these people. Nothing to say to anyone, really, even KD.

KD.

The reason for it all.

Steffie trudged along the sidewalk, wishing she had stopped long enough to get real boots instead of these dated Italian things. The thin leather did not protect her feet. And she wasn't wearing a coat. She looked like a homeless person in the pre-dawn darkness, and she knew if any of the residents of the Old Westside neighborhood peered out of their windows, they would wonder who was breaking curfew and why.

The walk to the house took three times longer than the shuttle ride. She stopped outside, astonished at how something that had loomed so large in her memory could look so small now.

The house had been built in 1910. It had two stories, a wide front porch, and a garage that had once been a barn tucked around the back. The large oak tree that covered the front lawn was half dead now. She and her brothers used to play around it.

KD had watched from the porch.

Lana hadn't even been born yet.

Steffie sighed, ran a hand through her messy hair, and walked up the path. It was cracked and smaller than she remembered. Her feet barely fit on the stones that her father had so carefully laid during the summer of her thirteenth year.

The memories were coming back.

She hated that.

She had thought she was beyond them.

She paused in front of the glassed in front door and raised a hand. But she didn't knock. No one should have to knock on the door to their childhood home. She brought her hand down, bypassed the primitive security system, and let herself in.

The house smelled of banana bread, lemon furniture polish and her father's cigars. The cigar scent was faint—almost a memory—, as if he hadn't lit up in a long time. A small shudder ran down her back. How many times had she come home from school to these smells? Sometimes the baked goods overlaying the polish were cookies, sometimes it was cake, but the house always smelled of baking. Her mother worked at home, and she always took a break by making something sweet.

It was a wonder she wasn't fat. She didn't know about her brothers. She hadn't seen them since she left home, and of course, hadn't heard from them.

KD couldn't get fat.

The grandfather clock that had sat in Wyton households since the mid-19th century bonged the half hour. The sound was familiar and unfamiliar.

Steffie jumped.

The household was asleep. She could feel it in the stillness, almost as if a part of her could hear the uneven breathing from a floor away.

The main staircase with its newel posts and its wooden banisters (now worth such a fortune that her parents actually should update their security system) wound toward the upstairs bedrooms. She wondered if hers was still as she remembered it, or if her parents had turned it into a guest room.

She gazed up the steps into the darkness. KD was up there. If Steffie had any courage, she would wake KD, have a short visit, and then leave.

If she had any courage.

But she had none. She wanted to put off seeing KD as long as possible.

She avoided the staircase, and crossed beside the built-in bookshelves. The living room's layout hadn't changed in fifteen years. She sank onto the couch, fluffed a pillow and leaned back.

Let them be surprised in the morning.

[9]

SHE WOKE TO her mother's face centimeters from hers. Her mother had aged naturally, with lines and age spots and skin blotchy from uneven sun exposure. Her hair had gone completely gray, and she wore glasses instead of having her eyes enhanced.

Enhancements had lost their charm, after KD.

Her nose ring remained, though, the tiny diamond stud Steffies' father had given her in lieu of an engagement ring.

"Stephanie?" Her mother asked, voice rising. "Sweetheart?"

Steffie blinked as if she were waking out of a sound sleep when in fact she had awakened the instant her mother sat down. One of the benefits of flopping, an instant wakefulness.

"Mother." She kept her voice cool, as if she had awakened to her mother's touch ever day for the last fifteen years.

"He found you then."

The answer was obvious, so Steffie did not grace the remark with a reply.

"Why didn't you contact us? We'd have booked your ticket."

"No need," Steffie said. She yawned and stretched. The couch was the best bed she'd had in weeks. "Can I use the shower?"

"Sure," her mother said. "Towels are—"

"Where they always are, I know," Steffie said. And so were the extra clothes, and the special linens, and KD.

KD.

"How is she?" Steffie asked.

"Dying," her mother said. The response was curt, as if it held both anger and embarrassment.

Or maybe Steffie was just reading that in.

"I didn't think that was possible," Steffie said, although she had suspected it was. She had suspected from the beginning.

"It was—you know—a long time ago. The technology was new."

Early adapters. She had never thought of her parents that way, but that's what they were.

Early adapters.

She wondered who set the trend.

She wondered who had coolhunted it.

She shivered.

"So what's happening?"

"Nothing you'd notice," her mother said. "It's all internal organ decay. On the cellular level, which makes sense, of course. Outside nothing has changed. She's still quite pretty. It's all so very Victorian—"

"The skin is an organ," Steffie said.

"But it's the most real of all of her parts," her mother said. "It didn't need much…"

She let her voice trail off.

"Tampering," Steffie said, and stood up. She was, for the first time, conscious of how filthy she was. How long had it been since she bathed? How long since she changed clothes? It didn't matter in New York. People were people were people there. But here, a single stain on the couch was an international incident.

"She wants to see you," her mother said. "You're all she's been asking for."

Steffie didn't want to hear that. She ran a hand through her hair, noticing this time not just the mess, but the grease as well. "After I clean up," she said. "She can wait one more hour."

"I guess," her mother said, although she sounded doubtful.

Steffie froze. "How long does she have?"

Her mother was still kneeling beside the couch. She looked like a supplicant in St. Patrick's. Her mother leaned her head on the couch's arm.

"I don't know," she said. "A month. Maybe more. We've been looking for you for a long time, Stef."

"It's amazing you found me at all," Steffie said, *and even more amazing that I showed up*, she thought, but the words didn't leave her mouth. There were some things, no matter how old she got, that she could never ever say.

10

THE SHOWER WAS a time warp. The same rusted showerhead, the same hard water, the same glass double doors. The soap was different, modern, softer and better for her skin.

She wondered if they had bought it for KD.

She found some of her old clothes in the extra clothes closet and put them on. They were too big, but the fabric was still good. The look wasn't even dated—not that it meant anything, since dated happened within an instant these days.

When she looked in the steamed mirror, she saw a face that she thought had disappeared when she left Ann Arbor the first time. Freshly scrubbed, innocent, eyes wide and blue and younger, it seemed, than KD's had been in that ancient family portrait.

She leaned her head against the silvered glass. She couldn't put it off any longer.

KD.

She had to see KD.

It was harder than it sounded. She hadn't been able to look at KD for years. Not since she understood what her parents had done to her older sister.

Steffie walked down the wide hallway, the thinning carpet hard and rough beneath her feet. She paused outside KD's door. How often she used to go into this room, first for comfort and then simply to be with her sister. As a child, Steffie had never understood KD's unchanging face. Only that KD was always as she expected, always as she had known she would be.

Until the anger started.

Maybe it had always been there. Maybe it became, in Steffie's tenth year, too much for KD to close in. But suddenly the beautiful perfect little girl had become every parent's nightmare: the tantrum-throwing screaming monster child. The child that was an embarrassment; the child that made the parents look like monsters themselves.

It was, Steffie realized much later, KD's only revenge.

Steffie pushed the door open. The room was filled with morning light. The white ruffled curtains were open to the backyard, the window closed because of the last of winter's chill. The canopied bed still sat against the north wall, but the ruffles were white now instead of pink. A comforter covered the bed, nearly hiding the small form in it.

KD.

Her ringlets were fanned across the pillow, her long lashes gracing her chubby cheeks. Her skin was, as her mother had said, still the color of porcelain, her small mouth still formed a perfect bow. KD had the face of a perfect child: the features that had been used by white portrait painters to portray angels and cherubs and saintly children for over a hundred and fifty years.

KD had been damned by fashion, by advertising, by perfection. Their parents had gotten caught up in the enhancement craze in the early teens, and had thought it would be wonderful to have a child forever. Not a child that would grow to become a rebellious teenager and then an angry adult. But a child, a real human child, forever.

The doctors hadn't even tried to talk them out of it. They had pushed for it, in fact, probably seeing all the credits multiplying in their accounts, not realizing that lawsuits, years later, would pull those credits right back out again.

Steffie grabbed the white straight-backed chair with a little heart carved in its back, and pulled it beside the bed. Then she touched her sister's hand for the first time in years.

KD's skin was soft, a child's skin. Steffie half expected it to smell of talcum. Instead, the room had a vague sweet odor, the odor of decay.

"KD," she said softly.

KD did not open her eyes. Steffie felt pain slice through her heart. Had she come too late then? She hadn't even known 12 hours ago that her sister was dying. It wouldn't be fair.

"KD," she said again, this time raising her voice slightly.

KD's eyelids flickered, then opened, revealing those round eyes of startling blue. Steffie had forgotten how rich the color was, a color that could not be duplicated by human beings, no matter how hard they tried.

Those eyes filled with tears. "Stef?"

Steffie nodded.

"They said they couldn't find you," KD said.

Steffie smiled, shrugged. "They were wrong." She left off the *as usual*. She felt the familiar—and old—incongruity she had always felt with her sister, the desire to protect a child, and the knowledge that KD was more savvy than most people gave her credit for.

KD's hand slipped out from under hers, and grabbed Steffie's first and middle fingers. "I'm glad you came," she said.

"Me, too," Steffie lied.

"No you're not," KD said. "You have a life. I've been trying to follow it, on the net, seeing which style change is yours. They never make it here, you know."

"I know," Steffie said.

"I think I found your trademark. You like flamboyance, don't you? No elegance for you. Someone taking risks. Someone willing to take that extra step that might be a success or a mistake."

Steffie smiled. That was her trademark. She had never thought of it in those terms before.

"I saw a woman talking about cool-hunting on the TV," KD said. "She said you couldn't pick a cool person without talking to them first, without knowing their attitudes, but I bet you can. I bet—"

"KD," Steffie said, not wanting to talk about herself. "I've got over four hundred million credits stashed in various accounts. I can get you treatments, things Mother and Dad can't afford. Maybe we can find a way to reverse this, or change it. Growth hormones, neuro-triggers, enhancement removal therapy, they're all expanding industries. There might be some solutions you don't know about—"

"So that I can grow big and strong like you?" KD's voice was dry. Steffie hadn't forgotten the anger, but she had forgotten the manifestation of it. The soft tones, the deceptively calm way KD had of speaking.

"So that you don't die." The words came out easier than Steffie had expected, given the pain that was slicing through her heart had moved into her throat.

KD removed her grip from Steffie's hand. "You know," KD said, "Mother and Dad never thought this through. They had the most perfect little girl, you know, but once their friends' children were grown, they stopped showing me off. I became a burden. It was like a failure on their part, that they had enough money to stop me here. We never left the house."

That was after Steffie had run away. "No," she said. "I didn't know."

"It didn't matter," KD said. "I didn't like playing any more which confused children, and adults didn't want to hold a conversation with me. They would turn away like I was a doll come to life."

Which was what she looked like. Permanent child enhancements were still done, but rarely now, and almost always by people whose kids would only make them a fortune when they were young. Child-models, child-actors, child-singers all had their bodies frozen in form, but not permanently any more. Even 'permanent' child enhancements lasted only as long as the child was worth something. Once the tastes changed—and they did, even in film, netvid, and advertising—then the child hyphens were able to grow up.

No one did child-child enhancements.

The common consensus now was that it was cruel.

"So I've been living on the nets. I thought I'd find you."

Steffie's throat was dry. She didn't know KD had been looking for her.

"I did find you, you know," KD said. "Only a ghost. Only a flicker. But I did find you. And you helped me. I wanted to tell you that."

Steffie shook her head. "I didn't do anything."

"Sure you did. Fashion betting. I kept wagering on you. It took some time, some net watching, but I had the time. I saw the style introduced and I bet on the adaptation time. I was good at it, Stef. Almost as good as you."

Steffie swallowed. She'd heard of fashion betting, but never practiced it. It seemed to her like a pastime of the rich, the idle, the people who could never do anything with their lives.

Like KD.

KD lowered her voice. "I have five million credits in an account in your name, Stef. It'd been more but for the doctors."

"The doctors?" Steffie asked.

KD nodded. Then she smiled. "Enhancements like mine don't reverse. It's too old."

It took a moment for Steffie to understand what KD had said. "Then you were trying—"

"To grow up," KD said. She closed her eyes, and for a moment it seemed as if she had gotten her wish. Her cheekbones were more prominent than they had ever been, her skin sallow. She looked like a tiny old lady on her deathbed.

Steffie ran a hand through her damp hair. She didn't want to walk through this emotional thicket. She had left because dealing with KD had torn her up. Because her family had focused only on KD the child, not KD the unhappy child-woman.

"You made this happen?" Steffie asked.

KD opened her eyes. Her smile was tiny, girlish, like a child who'd been caught playing with the wrong toys. "Growth hormones."

"How did you buy them? Don't you need Mom's permission?" Permanent children were always considered children in the eyes of the law. The assumption was that these beings were designed not to grow up, so no matter how much experience they accumulated, no matter how many years they had lived, they would never achieve adult status in the eyes of the world.

KD scrunched her pillow back. The movement looked difficult. The bones of her arms stuck out of what once had been plump cherubic flesh. "That's why I had to see you," she said, her voice at a whisper. "I used your name."

"What?" All the muscles in Steffie's back went rigid.

"I used your name." KD's eyes were wide. Her lower lip was trembling. "You weren't using it. And I needed a legal adult to fill out the forms, to give permissions and send in the e-papers. That's why the money's in your name."

"You used my name to what?" Steffie asked.

"To get me the appointments. To get me the treatments."

Steffie swallowed. If she had been here, she might have

helped. But she hadn't been here. She had left long ago. "All right. Why is that a problem?"

"Because I lied," KD said. A tear trembled at the tip of one of her lashes. "I said I got the enhancements less than twenty years ago."

"And that's important because—"

"The growth hormones don't work on enhancements like mine." Her voice rose into a wail. She did sound young. She acted young. But Steffie didn't know if that was because KD had been in this room for the past thirty years or because the enhancements did indeed keep her young.

"But you tried anyway."

"I read on-line that they just said that the hormones didn't work to keep us older ones in line. So I thought I could try it. But—" she rubbed the tear away with one small fist "—what no one said was that the hormones worked on people like me. They just worked wrong."

"Wrong?" Steffie asked. Her stomach was queasy. From the kitchen below rose the scents of coffee mixed with waffles.

"Wrong," KD said. "I'm aging, inside. Steffie, I have the heart of a 95 year-old woman, and it gets older every day. All the other organs are changing like that too."

"Except your skin."

"Even my skin, but not as fast. The enhancements didn't have to touch it much because it would stay young if the rest of me did."

"Isn't there something they can do to reverse this?" Steffie asked. "More enhancements, maybe? Something to block the hormones?"

"No," KD said. "Not with this kind of destruction. The

thing is, three weeks ago, I got legal notification for you that as my sister, you should have known the year I got enhanced. If I die, they'll go after you."

"After me? How?"

KD shrugged. "Misuse of information. Lying on government forms. Enough to hound you. To take your money. To freeze your identity."

Steffie kept her expression neutral. It didn't matter. She had enough identities. All it meant was that she would formally lose Stephanie Wyton-Brew. Whom she had already lost.

KD took her response for anger. She looked away.

"I wanted to grow up, Steffie." KD's voice was soft, plaintive. "You got to go out and see the world, all by yourself. I've never gone farther than Ann Arbor. I'm not even supposed to cross the street alone."

The complaint made the skin on Steffie's back crawl. She'd heard it all her life.

She was wrong about everything changing.

Here, nothing did.

She couldn't pay attention to that. She couldn't or she would go mad.

"Okay," Steffie said. "First things first. We see if we can find you some solutions. I know folks in companies with experimental treatments. Since we've already broken a few laws, we may break a few more and see if they'll send us some stuff that'll reverse this aging process. Then we'll find a doctor who'll work with you. We'll take it one step at a time."

"Will that work?" KD asked. Her voice was curious,

but her eyes weren't. There was something in them, something Steffie didn't recognize.

She shook it off. She hadn't seen KD in a long time. How could she pretend to understand her?

"There's only one way to find out if it'll work," Steffie said.

"Are you willing to try?" KD asked.

Steffie felt it, that familiar sensation that she had just been outmanuevered, outthought by a girl who couldn't get out of bed. But she didn't see how.

"I don't know," Steffie said.

"I won't beg," KD said.

"I'm not asking you to," Steffie said. But deep down, she almost wished KD would.

11

STEFFIE NEEDED TIME to think. She let her mother serve her waffles with fresh strawberries and real butter, coffee and fresh-squeezed orange juice, just as if this were a Sunday morning and Steffie had never left home. The kitchen was still the center of the house, and on this morning, it had on electric lights against the winter gloom. The cabinets were white, done in 1990s kitsch, the stove a flat top with a conventional interior. Only the refrigerator was new: a compact model that miniaturized food and expanded it upon removal.

Steffie said nothing about her family's penchant for keeping things small.

Her father sat at the head of the table, an e-paper open but unread beside him. Her mother was still making waffles in the stove's waffle-maker attachment. Dozens of waffles for only four people.

Steffie wondered how much food her mother discarded every day.

Her father was staring at her.

Fifteen years had diminished her father. His shoulders had hunched forward, his face had gone flabby, and his crew cut was an inch long, making him look as if he wore a brush on the top of his head. The hair had gone gray, just as his skin had gone a pale white. He looked like an old man, even though he wasn't.

She found herself staring back at him, chewing as she did so. She had forgotten that cooking was one of her mother's best skills. The waffles were wonderful; it was a shame most of them would be discarded. She knew half a dozen people in the park alone who could have lived on these waffles for a week.

"You shouldn'ta left," her father said finally, his voice grating on his throat, as if he didn't want the words to come out.

She shrugged, chewed a bit more, and swallowed. "I didn't want to stay here."

"KD needed you. She loved you. You were the only one she talked to."

"Maybe she'd have more friends if you let her out of the house," Steffie snapped.

"She's too ill," her mother said.

"She wasn't fifteen years ago," Steffie said.

Her father looked down at his e-paper. Her mother poured more batter into the waffle maker. Steffie took a sip of her orange juice, her heart pounding.

She set the glass down. "Look," she said, unable to stand the silence. She had grown up in this silence. It was a powerful thing, a wall she couldn't breach. Every time she brought up a topic that was forbidden, her parents would greet that topic with silence, pretending as if she hadn't even spoken, yet making her feel guilty for opening her mouth.

"Look," she said again. "You know what KD did."

"Some of it," her mother said.

"And you knew she implicated me to do it."

"Yes." That was her mother again, in a whisper. She shot a furtive glance at her husband, but he didn't look up. He was going to ignore this conversation if he could.

"And you still sent for me?" Steffie clenched a fist. "Why don't you take care of her? Or did you want her to die?"

"She won't die," her father said.

"Oh, just like she won't grow up?" Steffie asked. "Did you arrange that too?"

"No." Her mother put her hand on her father's shoulder. He covered it with his own. Steffie had forgotten that gesture, the gesture of unity from her childhood.

"We were hoping," her mother said, and her voice broke. She swallowed to cover the emotion, and then took a deep breath. "We were hoping you could help her."

"Me?" Steffie asked. "Why me?"

"Because she won't take our help."

Steffie looked at both of them. "Why not?"

Steffie's mother bit her lower lip. "She wants to take too many risks."

Obviously, Steffie thought. But said nothing. "So you want me to take the risks with her?"

"No," her mother said. "We thought you could talk her out of them."

"Me? Why me?"

"Because you loved her," her father said. "At least you did once."

"I felt sorry for her," Steffie said.

"You adored her," her mother said. "You followed her everywhere. And then when you got bigger, you carried her with you. She was your advisor, your best friend, your sister. Surely you remember."

Steffie remembered. And she remembered the late night conversations, the pounding of tiny fists against her chest, the way KD's cruel small fingers pinched Steffie's developing body, the symbol of the difference between them. She remembered it all, and the pain of it, the confusion she felt when her beloved sister had turned all her rage on Steffie because Steffie would grow up.

"I was a child," Steffie said.

"KD still is," her father said.

Steffie shook her head. "That's the thing you two never got, did you? The treatment you gave her did not leave her a child. She's an adult, but the law doesn't recognize it. Her appearance doesn't allow it. But her mind has grown, and changed, and learned. Just like yours has."

"You haven't spent these years with her," her mother said. "You don't know—"

"Of course I know," Steffie said. "It was happening even as I was growing up. It's hard when your sister, who is supposed to be a perpetual three year-old has a better vocabulary and more knowledge of human nature than you do."

"The doctors said that would happen," her father said. "There'd be some learning, of course, but other things would always be beyond her."

"Like making a living? Like thinking for herself?"

Her mother nodded.

"How do you think she paid for the treatments?" Steffie said. "She didn't just implicate me. She broke into my systems, used my name and ID."

"There've been movies about that," her mother said. "I could do that."

"Could you fashion gamble?" Steffie asked.

"What?" her mother said.

"Fashion gamble," Steffie said. "KD made 5 million credits fashion gambling. That's how she planned to pay for everything. She has her own money. She wants out of here. And the only way she can get out is to grow up."

"It's too late for that now," her mother said.

Steffie sighed. Fifteen years, fifteen years of independence, of no contact with these people, and the instant she walked in the door, the old irritations returned. Her parents' refusal to acknowledge what they had done to their own daughter and the consequences of it. The effect it had on the family.

The effect it had on KD.

"No," Steffie said. "It might not be too late. We have five million credits to work with and that buys a lot of treatments."

Steffie didn't tell them about her credits. She would probably need those, if she did something wrong, if she made a wrong move.

"The problem is," she continued, "that KD won't try any treatment, not as long as she stays small."

"She wouldn't be KD if she grew," her father said.

Steffie turned toward him. His head was still bent.

There were dandruff flakes in his bristly hair. The food Steffie had eaten sat like a lump in her stomach.

"You would rather have KD die?" Steffie asked.

"Seems to me," her father said, "that KD will die either way."

"Childhood was never meant to be permanent," Steffie said. "*Nothing* in this world is meant to be permanent."

Her father did not answer. He drew his silence around him like a blanket, a shield against Steffie's words.

"You can help her, then," her mother said, ignoring the interchange. "You know what to do."

"I can try," Steffie said, regretting the words the instant that she spoke them. "But you'll have to help me in return."

"Anything," her mother said.

"I won't even do anything until you agree to let KD grow up."

"No," her father said.

Her mother squeezed her father's shoulder. Steffie saw him wince in pain. "Whatever it takes," her mother said. "Whatever it takes."

[12]

HER PARENTS' COMPUTER was in the den. Her mother hovered behind her as she went inside, and faced a machine the size of a mirror, an antique she remembered from her childhood. She wondered if this was the machine KD had used to track her coolhunting, to make her five million credits, to gamble on fashion. She hadn't seen anything in KD's room, but that meant nothing. Computers could be small as a fingernail these days. Steffie had even coolhunted a couple of full body interfaces and tiny tattoos that were full performance machines. The craze had lasted ten days, one of her longest and best.

"Codes and passwords?" Steffie asked as she put her hand on the leather chair. It felt the same, cool to the touch, the leather softened with age.

"They're programmed in."

Steffie wanted to warn her, to say that such things were irresponsible. But when had her parents been sensible or

54

responsible? They had only appeared so. And appearances were so important to them all.

"Scans?" Steffie asked.

"Retinal, palm, full face for some things," her mother said.

Steffie sighed. She could go around the scans, but she didn't want to. She didn't know who was monitoring the house, if anyone, but she didn't want to do anything too suspicious. Looking for a cure for KD was probably unusual enough, but easily explainable. Going around security systems, well, that was a felony, and one they would most certainly blame on her.

"Okay," Steffie said, not sitting down. "Get me on."

Her mother glanced at her, then went to the chair. It sagged under her weight. She put her hands on the keyboard, typing in codes. "What system?" her mother asked.

"Excuse me?" Steffie said.

"What net do you want?" Her mother asked, clarifying the question.

"Anything," Steffie said. She wasn't going to search for research—her family could do that—she was going to hunt. What she did best. Only she had never done it this way. "On second thought, go to one of the difficult ones. Better to have too much security than not enough."

Her mother typed. The machine was old enough to have a clicking keyboard, something that grated on Steffie. She preferred silence, required silence in fact when she typed anything. If she had to have sound, she used a voice activated system.

Then her mother eased out of the chair. The ancient

monitor blurred a tunnel that should have been an automatic VR view. Steffie sat down The chair was warm from her mother.

"Thanks," Steffie said, and began to work.

The medical boards were encoded and filled with garbage: people discussing their symptoms, asking for help with common problems, debating the financial practicalities of curing old age. The fundamental arguments, the ones she had heard all her life. Only she had known, as did anyone with a brain, that if they could create children like KD, they could stop people from dying. They could arrest them at any age—35, 50, it didn't matter—but they refused because of the burden it would place on society.

Funny how perpetual children were not a burden when older, more experienced people were.

Hunting in here was not like walking the streets. It was more complex. But like streets, the attention to detail was the same. She wasn't looking for a paper on KD's arrested development or on growth hormones. Steffie was searching chat areas, listening to live conversations while she was digging through the research boards.

Listening for that single comment, looking for the silence that implied more knowledge than the user was willing to admit to. Whenever she found a name, she cross-referenced it with the Copyright Office's annual publication of the names of people who applied for patents.

By evening she had a headache, and her eyes ached from looking at material designed for systems that lasted hours instead of years. Her mother, who had apparently left the room sometime that morning, brought in three sandwiches, some homemade potato chips, and a mochachino, something that no one had made in so many years the taste actually invoked childhood—a small dinner party where Steffie at age 3, the only time she was KD's contemporary, got to taste her first caffeinated beverage.

And hated it.

She smiled at the memory, took a sandwich, and felt her mouth water at the prospect of eating choice-cut beef. Her parents had never skimped on food. They had skimped on other things, but never food.

Her mother returned some time later to take the plate.

"Steffie," she said softly.

Her voice sounded like an explosion in the tight room. Steffie, who'd been following two chats and cross-reading patents, listening to on-line medical radio, and searching the drug listings, jumped.

"KD?" she asked.

"No change," her mother said. "How are you doing?"

"Fine," Steffie said, in a tone that brooked no more interruption.

Her mother watched her for a moment. When it became clear that Steffie wasn't going to say anything more, her mother took the empty mochachino glass, and left the sandwiches. Steffie grabbed another as she returned her attention to her work.

Twelve non-stop hours later, she had learned a lot of things, some she didn't want to know. Not surprisingly, but something she had not thought of, was that KD was not alone. Large groups of "children" haunted net space, some in groups, some individually. Most were using their parents' systems illegally, using illegal identities, and playing the same tricks KD had.

Steffie wondered how much of this KD knew, and how much she had used before she got ill.

Or even if some of these groups had helped her take Steffie's identity, helped her find the doctor who had been willing to work on her without a certified adult present.

But all of those were questions for later, questions Steffie might never get answered. And although they were irritating, they weren't really relevant.

Not considering what else she found.

Ninety-seven patents had been issued to help the "children" grow. Another fifty-two had been issued to cope with diseases of the non-aging, and twenty-five had been issued to deal with the effects of growth hormones on the early adapters.

Twenty-five.

And of those twenty-five, twenty had received permission to do experiments on humans.

Of those twenty, ten had completed the studies.

Of those ten, only one had "children" who survived.

Only one.

At that point, Steffie had stopped and put her face in her hands. His treatment had been effective, but it had done something the parents opposed, and they had shut him down.

It had left the growth hormones intact.

The early adaptive child had arrived at his office, sickly on the edge of death, just like KD, and had left a full adult, with years ahead of them. The legal problems had been startling. The new adults had no legal standing since they were registered as permanent children, and their parents, who had uniformly not approved the treatment (the "children" had gotten it as they had gotten the growth hormones, through theft of adult documentation), had sued.

The doctor was no longer practicing. His bio said that he worked in the CUNY system as a biology teacher, and saw no one.

Especially not people like KD.

It seemed a bit too pat.

Steffie ate the last sandwich, and stared at the screen. Her eyes hurt, her head ached, and her shoulders were so tight that she pulled a muscle.

The sandwich was stale, the bread hardened by its exposure to air.

Her father would never approve. He would rather have KD die. Steffie closed her eyes.

KD, of course, would be excited about it.

Her mother would not take a stand, and Steffie would be in the middle, as always.

And that was assuming the doctor would work with them, that he would give up his safe little job in the CUNY system, and break the law to help KD.

Why had Steffie come back here?

Why did she think she could save her sister's life?

She had never been able to before.

THE HOUSE WAS asleep when she finally stood up. She stretched and her spine cracked. It had been a long time since she spent a day in a chair, not moving. Usually she was always on the move, always doing something different, always finding a way to keep herself busy, to be creative

But not to think.

Never to think.

Or remember.

She remembered so much about this house. She remembered its rhythms, the silent hush it got when all the occupants but her were sleeping. She remembered the way the ceiling groaned in a harsh wind, the soft spot in the center of the fifth stair up, the wobbly spindle near the top of the banister.

And most of all, she remembered KD.

—*You gotta help me. You're bigger. You could take me on the shuttle*—

—*I'm not old enough.*

—They won't have to know. And then when I'm on my own, I'll find a way to repay you.

—You can't be on your own, KD.

—Then you can live with me. You'll be my adult. Only you won't have to supervise me because I won't need it. You'll do that, won't you, Stef? Think of all the times I helped you...

And most of all, she remembered the night she ran away. KD was still an accepted oddity, then. A member of an elite group, a prized possession, a status symbol not unlike expensive jewels or a house in the country. KD had given one of her best performances at dinner: a combination of precocious intelligence, and nauseating cuteness. She had conversed with the visiting German professor in his own language about the upcoming celebration of thirty years of his country's unity, and then, by request, she had lisped her way through a lullaby. She had cuddled on command with their father's boss, a childless woman who always treated KD like a stray animal, and then she had graciously accepted the small gifts of toys some of her parents' regular visitors had brought.

The toys got tossed into the corner of her room, and she had run to Steffie's, sobbing in her arms. Steffie had held her, understanding KD's humiliation for the first time, and the futility of it all.

And she had confronted their parents like she would have to confront them now, and they had told her she would never understand.

Never.

They were right.

Oh, she knew the history, but it never made sense to

her. They had lost their first child, a girl, of some sudden onset disease that she should have been inoculated for, but somehow wasn't. (They always skipped over this part, as if it were someone else's fault, not their own.) By then, they had already had KD. Shortly after their first child died, they decided to prevent KD's loss. They decided to have a child forever, so they not only inoculated her against all childhood diseases, they also inoculated her against adulthood.

And the treatment had been so awful, they decided not to do it to the rest of their children. But KD had given them courage to have other children. She had given them their life back.

So they used to say, back when KD was their status symbol, their performing monkey.

Before society decided what they did was no longer fashionable, and just a little bit wrong.

[14]

BY THE TIME Steffie finished the sandwich, she knew what she had to do. She couldn't run this time. She had chosen to come back on her own. She had chosen to face the heartache, to see KD this last time. And in seeing her sister, in seeing what she had become, what she had done to herself just to try to have a normal life, Steffie could no longer leave.

KD deserved the chance to live her life, any life, on her own terms. Not on her parents' terms. Not on Steffie's.

On her own.

In her searches, Steffie had found the exact costs of the doctor's legal bills, and the extent of his garnishment at CUNY. He had never made much money. He had done this for a reason not covered in the gossip trades, a reason known only to him. But he was in deep and severe debt, and he could no longer practice his real trade. He had taken the job at CUNY out of desperation, wasting his talents teaching children for less than one-fiftieth of what he made before.

It bothered her that the information had been easy to find. It made her leery. But not leery enough to ignore him.

She offered to pay his legal bills, current and future, if he promised to treat KD. She sent this to him in encrypted e-mail, routed through half a dozen sources, and out of one of her dormant names.

Traceable, she supposed, but she doubted it. The amount of work would keep him busy for the next two weeks.

And that was if he were an expert in computers, which he clearly was not.

His response was startlingly immediate.

He accepted.

[15]

SOME THINGS BECAME clear. The doctor was not what he seemed. The credits he wanted were too high; the address he gave was far from CUNY, and he offered to provide the adult KD with proper identification.

Steffie accepted it all. She had worked the seamier sides of the street too long to be shocked at the lengths people went to in order to get their work done.

Maybe her parents would have been shocked.

Maybe KD would have.

But Steffie knew:

Sometimes you had to do whatever it took.

HER PARENTS NO longer slept in the same room. That was a change, and one Steffie had not expected. Her mother had taken the twins' room for herself. Only one bed remained, and a few of the twins' things, but her mother's presence there did not look temporary. Her books were piled on the nightstand, her clothing littered the floor. A small entertainment unit with everything from computer remote to VR to good old fashioned television was hooked to the foot of the bed.

The faint nightlight, a glass ball that had a phosphorescent glow, which Steffie had always associated with her parents' room was on the dresser.

Steffie had stumbled into this room by accident, looking for her old penlight to carry into her parents' bedroom, not expecting her mother to be inside.

Her mother slept on her back with one arm flung above her head. She looked younger than Steffie had ever seen her —a combination of the soft light and the relaxation of sleep.

Steffie saw herself in her mother's features, the long narrow face, the small mouth. She saw KD too, the promise of what KD would be.

Would have been.

Steffie went to her mother's side, crouched, and touched her mother's shoulder. When she didn't wake, Steffie's heart started to pound. She knew her mother was all right; she could hear the rhythmic breathing. But she wondered if her mother had taken anything to help her sleep, and felt the old frustration rise even though she didn't yet have proof.

The impracticality of it. A sick child—a sick person—Steffie still had to mentally correct herself, and she hated it —in the house, and her mother took some kind of chemical to help her sleep.

Steffie shook her mother's shoulder harder than she initially intended. Her mother's eyes blinked, and her eyebrows came together in a frown.

"Stephanie?" Her mother's voice was slurred with sleep.

"Wake up, Mother, I need to talk to you," Steffie said.

"KD. Is she—?"

"I haven't been in her room yet. I've come to see you."

Her mother was waking up more completely now. She slid back toward the pillows and pushed her hair out of her face. "You found something," she said in a normal voice.

"Yes," Steffie said. "A doctor who knows how to help KD."

"How much will it cost?"

More than Dad wants to pay, Steffie nearly answered,

but decided at that moment not to say anything. "I'll worry about the cost."

"She's still our responsibility," her mother said.

Steffie shook her head. "You involved me."

"We'll take care of it," her mother said.

"No." Steffie was adamant. Her mother looked confused. Steffie wasn't about to admit the real reason for her generosity.

She didn't want her parents to interfere.

When it became clear that her mother would not accept Steffie's argument, Steffie said simply, "I guess I owe her for running away."

Her mother said nothing to that. She adjusted the blankets, then reached over and clicked on the bedside light. Steffie blinked at the sudden brightness.

"What do we do?" her mother asked.

"We get her out of here," Steffie said.

Her mother stared at her. "I'd like to take her."

"And what will you tell Dad?"

Her mother looked away.

"What is it?" Steffie asked. "Why is he so unwilling to let her grow up?"

"I don't know," her mother whispered. But Steffie could tell she lied.

[17]

AFTER SHE LEFT her mother's room, Steffie stood in the hallway for a moment. If she was going to back out, this was her only chance. Her only chance to escape the house, and never be seen again.

But KD's skeletal face would haunt her. KD's voice had, over the years, bemoaning Steffie's freedom, Steffie's size, Steffie's life. Steffie didn't sleep much as it was. She wouldn't be able to sleep at all if she abandoned KD now.

She opened the door to KD's room—and thought for a moment that KD had given her a reprieve.

The silence was odd. And almost terrifying. Then KD took a loud shuddery breath, and Steffie realized that her sister was still alive.

Steffie sat on the bed and touched KD's shoulder, much as she had touched her mother's.

KD's eyes opened immediately. "I thought you'd be gone," she said.

"I found someone to help you," Steffie said, a bit more rigidly than she had planned.

"Dr. Doom?" Then when Steffie frowned, KD added, "The guy who holds the patent?"

"You knew about him?"

"Sure. I know my way around the boards."

Steffie felt a trembling deep inside. Nothing changed. KD was playing her again, touching her sympathies and then throwing them back in her face.

"I spent hours searching for him," Steffie said, wondering how she managed to keep her voice so soft when all she wanted to do was scream at KD.

"Took me three days," KD said. "You are better than me."

"You could have saved me the time," Steffie said, "and just told me about him."

"Wouldn'ta worked," KD said. "You never believe anything you don't find on your own."

There was too much truth in that statement.

"We have a date to meet him," Steffie said. "And a place. Are you willing to go through with this?"

"I won't do it," KD said, "Unless it allows me to grow."

"It's one of the side effects," Steffie said. "But you already knew that."

KD smiled. "I already knew that."

"That's why you brought me here. Not to inform me of anything, but to take you to this man."

"Yes," KD said.

"Why? Mom would have taken you."

"No, she wouldn't," KD said. "I'm all she has left."

Steffie felt the world spin into place. She had left, run

away. Her brothers and Lana were gone, too. Steffie had noted, on that family page, that none of them had been home in years either. Her parents' children grew up and away, and didn't just leave the nest.

They had abandoned it.

KD couldn't, not legally and not physically.

"I asked Mom to help me smuggle you out of here. Was that wrong?"

KD shook her head. "Unlike Dad, Mom still has a sense of what's right. She only acts on it when pushed, but she can be pushed."

Somehow that didn't reassure Steffie. "How do I push her?"

KD smiled. "I think you already did."

STEFFIE SNUCK AROUND the house, preparing for the trip. The first shuttle didn't leave until 6 a.m. She couldn't sleep, so she went through her own closet with an eye for cool. Most of the clothes brought back memories: the blue and white dress with the sailor collar that she had bought with her own money; the silk sweater that had been too hot for her first date; a pair of Levi's, true Levi's, that dated from the mid-1950s and were worth their weight in gold. She wondered how many other treasures she'd find in this house, old once-fashionable things that had been out of style so long that they had become valuable antiques.

Probably nothing from the modern era would become an antique. Fashion came and went too quickly. It didn't have time to linger; the word antique was slowly beginning to mean something over a month old.

She chose an outfit from her closet to wear back to New York. The top was a pale peach tent shirt with a faux paisley pattern; the bottoms were a pair of brown gauze pants. She kept her boots—she couldn't walk far without them—but she tossed a pair of sandals into her stuff for safe keeping. She grabbed an old shoulder pouch, filled it, and slipped it over one arm. Then she pinned her hair on both sides of her head with matching ribbon barrettes.

For a day, at least, she wouldn't be Steffie Storm-warning. She'd be KD's sister and the responsible adult for an important operation.

All they had to do was get out of the house before her father woke up.

Steffie had asked KD why their father didn't want her to change, didn't want her to grow. Their father, more than their mother. And KD had looked at her with those old, old eyes in that still-young face: *Don't you see what a failure he is? I remind him of the days when the world still had possibilities.*

Steffie had been thinking about that statement since she had come to her old room. It rang something within her; it made an emotional kind of sense. It was hard for her to think of her father as a failure: he had a job, he had this wonderful home, and he had a family. But his job was inherited, a tenured position he had taken from his father at the University of Michigan. The house was inherited too, and paid for. It had never cost their family a dime to live inside. Her parents hadn't remodeled. They hadn't even bought new furniture, except for the children's rooms.

The only thing they had spent money on was KD and she had been a victory for a time. A fashionable statement, a symbol of wealth and power—look! We can stop time!—and a luxury.

But it got him nothing except a bitter woman in a

child's body, a woman tied to him and his inadequate life forever. His family was in ruins; his wife no longer slept with him, his second oldest daughter had run away the night before she graduated from high school, and the remaining children were gone, never to return.

When he died what would he have to show for his life but KD? She was the only stable thing in it.

KD, the house, and the job.

Only KD was his own.

His very own.

Steffie stood. She didn't know what it felt like to have something of her own. She flopped, bought clothes when she needed them, and discarded them when she was done. The only things she owned were her names, her accounts, and her contacts.

Her brains.

And her eye.

Nothing else.

It was strange to return to this place of history and see clothes so old that she could remember the first time she wore them, remember being fourteen and full of hope.

Even then she had sensed her parents' bitterness. Both of them, bitter at growing older, at living their lives like their parents had, at not stepping out of the confines of this simple house.

Much like KD.

Did their father want KD to be stuck here because he was?

She glanced at the room with its off-white walls and familiar cracks. She couldn't imagine what the last fifteen years would have been like here, staying through the harsh winter, seeing the same people.

Watching KD remain the same.

Day after day after day.

Time passed and no one noticed.

No one noticed at all.

[19]

STEFFIE MADE HER way down the stairs like she had as a teenager on that last night, walking along the wooden sides, avoiding the creaks. Her mother sat at the base of the steps, cradling KD in a blanket. KD was too large for her mother. Large and heavy, like any three year-old. Big enough to walk on her own.

But KD could no longer do that.

For the first time, Steffie saw fear in her mother's eyes.

"She'd found this guy on her own," Steffie whispered.

"Stop," KD said.

"KD?" Her mother's voice held very real pain. "Is this true?"

Over the edge of her blanket, KD shot Steffie a killing look. "Yes," KD said.

"Why didn't you tell me? I'd have taken you. We wouldn't've had to wait."

Steffie's mouth opened slightly. She hadn't expected

this, her mother willing to do anything, even something vaguely illegal, to keep KD alive.

"Shh," KD said. "Dad will hear you."

But Steffie understood now. KD was using their father as a way not to answer the question. "Why did you wait?" Steffie asked.

KD closed her eyes. "You wouldn't have taken me, Mom. Dad would have stopped you."

Her mother put her head against KD's. "I want you to live."

"I know," KD said, in a resigned voice. "You want me to stay the same."

"Is that so wrong?" her mother asked.

KD didn't answer. Steffie couldn't. She cleared her throat.

"Do you want to call this off?" Steffie asked, her mouth suddenly dry, not knowing if she were addressing the question to her mother or her sister.

KD's eyes opened, large circles on her tiny face. "This is my only chance, Steffie," she said.

Steffie knew that. Their mother cradled KD closer. "We don't have much time," she said. "Your father will be down shortly after sun-up, wanting his coffee."

Like he had ever since Steffie could remember.

"All right," Steffie said, the knot in her stomach growing. "Let's go."

THE FAMILY HAD bought their car before Steffie had
been born. It was an old gas model, its combustion system
redesigned in the mid-aughts to accommodate new fuel
regulations. Steffie's parents had kept the car in pristine
condition; like KD its value came in preserving its
appearance.

Steffie's mother handed KD to Steffie, and climbed in
the driver's seat. KD was heavier than Steffie expected, all
dead weight and rubbery skin. No natural skin felt that
way, as if it were made of stuffed plastic, but then nothing
about KD was natural.

Steffie slipped into the passenger side, unwilling to put
her sister in the special seat in the back. KD was so weak
she could no longer sit on her own. No sense in even
trying.

The drive to the shuttle stop on the quad would be
short. But not as short as the shuttle ride itself. KD closed
her eyes. Her face looked drawn. It had that translucent

quality that Steffie had only seen before in the homeless who slept in the park.

The ones who were about to die.

Steffie shuddered. What had she gotten herself into? She felt absurdly guilty, found herself thinking if she had been more accessible, then her family would have found her sooner and she would have arrived before KD got so sick.

But much of KD's illness, all of it in fact, had been caused by KD. KD and her desire to be like everyone else. When she could never ever be.

Steffie looked down to see KD staring at her. KD smiled weakly. Steffie made herself smile back, even though she didn't want to. Even though she felt trapped, alone, and completely out of her depth.

Her mother backed the car up and drove the few short blocks to the university. The three of them traveled in silence. Amazing how, after being family, after not seeing each other, after facing such a crisis, they still had nothing to say to one another. Since she returned they had never once asked Steffie about the particulars of her work, or even if she enjoyed her job. They didn't ask where she lived, if she had a lover, if she had children.

Everything was lost in the focus on KD.

As usual.

Her mother pulled the car into the shuttle parking area. The shuttle was already on the ground, perched like a black bird in the quad, barely visible through the gap between the forty-year old dorms. When the designers of the college residential area had designed the space, they hadn't realized that all of the pleasant, green, park-like land would eventually be multi-purposed: shuttle landing spots, aircar maneuvers, and regularly scheduled volleyball games between the students.

KD pushed herself up on her thin arms and stared at the shuttle. She coughed once, and swallowed hard, but not before Steffie saw blood.

"Looks like it's ready," their mother said.

Steffie looked at the new reddish tint to KD's lips. "You know," she said to her mother, "that there are no guarantees."

"I know," her mother said. She ran a hand over KD's thinning hair. "I'll miss you, baby."

"She means I might die, Mom," KD said. "She doesn't want you to blame her."

Their mother looked at Steffie over KD's head. It was too late: they already blamed her. They blamed her for leaving, for growing up, for being a different person from them. Her parents had kept KD the way they wanted her, and they couldn't do that with their other children.

Now Steffie was taking KD away.

Maybe forever.

"You could come with us, Mom," Steffie said. "You might get back before Dad even knows you're gone."

Her mother shook her head.

"KD could use the support."

"I don't need it," KD said. "This is an adventure."

"You go," her mother said. "Do what you can." Then she kissed KD on the top of the head, and pushed Steffie's arm. Away from her. Get out of the car, the movement said. There was no affection, no attempt at it.

Steffie got out, cradling KD.

"KD," their mother said, and there was desperation in her voice. "I love you."

KD sighed silently. Steffie felt her body move. "I love you too, Mom," KD said, her words sweet, her tone in complete contradiction to the sudden tension in her body. "Thanks for bringing us here."

"We're going to miss the shuttle," Steffie said.

"Send us news," their mother said.

Steffie nodded and headed for the shuttle. She mounted the small ramp, punched her ticket code, and climbed inside without turning to wave at their mother. Steffie didn't want another look at her, or at the quad, or at Ann Arbor itself.

This time, as in the time before, she hoped she would never have to go back. If this treatment worked, KD could come home on her own.

If she chose to come home at all.

This shuttle had twenty-five seats and all but two were full. New York was still a business hub, although not as important as it had once been, and more people were willing to take five minutes out of their day to head there first thing in the morning.

Steffie kept KD's head covered in the blanket, not wanting people to gawk at her older sister. Not wanting people to remember them.

Or her.

She slipped into one of the empty seats, only to have KD croak, "Window."

Steffie sighed and moved to the other seat. "You can't really see out of these things," she said. "They're only for being on the ground."

"Don't tell me any more," KD said. She eased out of the blanket, letting it fall aside, and peered out the window, looking, for the first time since Steffie returned, like the little girl she was meant to be. "You know all this stuff. I want to discover it."

The words were strong, but the voice wasn't. Steffie wondered how much the trip had already taken out of KD, and how much more there was to take.

One more passenger arrived and took their original seat. Then the automatic straps buckled them all into place, including KD, holding her against Steffie's chest. They took off.

Steffie closed her eyes, but she didn't really doze. Five minutes wasn't long enough for an effective nap. Besides, it was hard with KD squirming on her lap, trying to see everything, trying to memorize everything, not afraid to show her complete and total awe at her surroundings.

Steffie had never shown such awe, not even on her first shuttle ride. In those days, it had been too important for her to keep her own aura of cool, not to let anyone know that she was interested in something, frightened of something, enjoying something.

KD had no sense of propriety, no sense of how she appeared in public.

Steffie guessed it didn't matter. People perceived KD as a child. She could get away with anything.

Except the things she wanted to get away with.

The shuttle landed on its own pad on top of Grand Central Station. Steffie cursed silently. She had forgotten to ask for a specific landing point, one closer to the address the doctor had given her. The restraints came off, and KD still leaned against her.

"Wow," KD whispered. "We're here?"

"Yes," Steffie said. She'd need another aircab, and she'd have to decide how close she wanted to be let off. She couldn't submit KD to too much of New York. It was difficult for those with strong constitutions.

KD didn't have much strength left.

Steffie waited until the other passengers got off the shuttle, then she carried KD out. KD's blanket trailed slightly, and KD had her arms around Steffie's neck. Her eyes were too bright, her cheeks had an unnatural flush, and she was looking around as if she had been invited to heaven and was being given a tour by God himself.

The landing platform was hot. Two more shuttles, probably the LA and Dallas ones, were resting nearby, passengers disembarking. A man, slender and tan, glanced at Steffie and smiled.

She did not smile back.

The crowd made her nervous. She didn't know how to be around a crowd when she wasn't coolhunting, when she wasn't working. She cradled KD close, and made her way to the aircab stand.

Five men in business suits complete with pocket watch/computer/phone attached to their ample waists waited at the stand. Three women in platforms two feet high, and an elderly person whose gender Steffie couldn't identify also waited. A woman in an official green uniform used a soundless whistle to summon the taxis.

If Steffie didn't gain her sympathy, they'd waste ten minutes here.

She approached cautiously, then pulled the blanket down from KD's head. "Ma'am," Steffie said, doing her best to sound like she still was from Michigan. "My daughter—"

"Get in line!"

"Who do ya think you are?"

"We were here first!"

The shouts came from behind her. She knew then that she had a chance. Those people would not have yelled if they didn't already feel as if they had lost a position in line.

"My daughter is ill," Steffie said. "I'm trying to get her to a specialist."

The woman looked at both of them. KD was obviously ill. Steffie could see that reflected in the woman's eyes. "Shoulda told the shuttle to set you close."

"I didn't know you could," Steffie said.

The woman shook her head. Then she whistled for an aircab, held one of the large men back, and let Steffie and KD slide in.

"Thanks," KD said, voice a rasp.

"Get better," the woman said and signaled the taxi to move with her arm.

Steffie leaned back in the seat then gave the driver an address on the Lower East Side. He circled Grand Central and then took off as if an entire raft of police were after him.

KD watched from the comfort of Steffie's arms. "Is it always like this?" she asked.

"No," Steffie said. "Usually people aren't that friendly."

Then she realized that she didn't have to lie to KD. KD would never return here. She would never be a tourist alone on these mean streets. KD could know that New

Yorkers generally were friendly. The problem was that you sometimes couldn't tell the friendly ones from the unfriendly ones.

"There's no trees," KD said.

"We're going the wrong way for trees." Steffie cradled her sister close. She had never expected KD here. Suddenly she felt as if KD were a three-year-old child, subject to all the horrors the city could present.

"And it's old. Those buildings are older than the ones in Ann Arbor."

"Dirtier," Steffie said.

Her responses didn't diminish KD's enthusiasm. "I've never been in an aircab before."

Or on a shuttle.

Or in a state outside of Michigan.

Or in a city that was a world unto itself.

KD had never had sex, never held a job, never fallen in love. KD hadn't lived a life at all.

And she was dying.

"Why do they call him Doctor Doom?" Steffie asked, afraid of the answer.

For the first time, KD took her eyes off the city. She looked at Steffie, and Steffie got a hint of what KD in an adult's body would look like. Beautiful, menacing, intimidating as hell.

"Because," KD said. "No one ever comes back."

Steffie's stomach flopped. She was taking her sister to meet death. KD had known it all along.

"I can't do this," Steffie said.

"Sure you can," KD said. "He doesn't always kill people. A lot of them never return to their parents because they're cured. And big. They can have their own lives."

"I'm not liking what I hear," Steffie said.

"It's not your choice," KD said. But there was a bravado in her voice. It was Steffie's choice. She was the legal adult even though she was the younger of the two. It was a fiction between them that KD had any control at all.

"You don't care what he does to you?" Steffie asked.

KD leaned against her. She was tiring visibly, the pallor of her skin growing. "I care," KD said. "I care very much."

[21]

THE ADDRESS DOCTOR DOOM had given her was
on one of those narrow sidestreets with so many rules about
aircabs that most avoided the place. The driver let them off
on a corner, and Steffie walked the rest of the way.

KD was too tired to move. Once Steffie looked down at
her, and KD had smiled weakly, but she had said nothing.
When they reached the address, a man came out a steel
doorway. He stopped in the middle of the sidewalk, and his
gaze met Steffie's.

He seemed to know who they were, but then, how
could he miss? How many other women walked through
this part of the city with a three year-old child—or someone
who looked like one—in their arms?

"You're going to go through with this?" he asked, and
he sounded almost disappointed.

"Yes," Steffie said.

He sighed and went to the door. "I am no miracle work-
er," he said. He was looking at KD.

"They call you Doctor Doom," she said hoarsely.

For the first time, he smiled. It made him look younger, in his mid-forties, a cascade of laugh lines forming on his careworn face. "They do," he said. "And they are right."

[22]

THE FRONT PART of his rented space served as a reception area. From the makeshift kitchen in the corner and the ratty look of the couch, Steffie suspected it also doubled as his home. He never did give them his real name, although Steffie knew it. Instead, he led her to the back room, which looked shinier, newer, and cleaner than any hospital she had ever been in.

Now the doubts she had felt when she discovered him made sense. That had only been his screen persona, designed to scare away those who were not serious. This was not a man who taught at CUNY, who had exorbitant legal bills. This was a man who made a living off people like KD.

"The authorities know about me," he said. "They will have your e-mail by now."

"Then why don't they come for you?"

He smiled again. "They tried. But there is no law yet

89

against saving lives, now is there? Only a lack of courage on the part of the government and the normal facilities."

"Do you save lives?" Steffie asked.

"Sometimes," he said. A man came out of a side room that Steffie hadn't even realized was there. This man was slender and younger than Steffie. He took KD from her, and placed her on a steel table in the center of the room.

"There are no legal bills, are there?" Steffie asked.

Dr. Doom smiled at her. "There are always legal bills," he said.

She no longer wanted to leave KD there. She no longer trusted him with KD, if she ever had.

KD was scanning the room, her small head turning.

"This is a mistake," Steffie said to her.

KD eased up on her elbows. The whites of her eyes were a dull yellow, and the blood was back in the corner of her mouth. "It's a chance, Steffie," she said. And then, with a last burst of strength, she added, "It's my choice."

Her choice.

Steffie crossed her arms. KD was right, no matter what the law said. It was her choice. And she had stated it over and over. If she had to remain the way she was, she wanted to die. If there was no chance of change, there would be no survival.

"Can you help her?" Steffie asked.

Dr. Doom looked at her. His mouth was a thin line, his eyes wide. He did not have the blustery confidence that most doctors had.

"We can only try," he said.

[23]

DURING THE OPERATION, she went outside. The day was sunny with a hint of muggy; the city smelled of garbage as it always did.

She was surprised to realize that she had missed it.

Spring was in full swing. Soon it would be summer.

Summer was her best time of year.

She sat down on a stoop at a nearby building, and brought her knees up to her chest. She wrapped her arms around them, trying to seek comfort from herself. What would she do with KD? If KD died, then Steffie'd have to take the body back to Ann Arbor, and admit to her parents that she had failed. She knew her mother would be upset, but she wasn't certain about her father. He hadn't wanted an adult KD, and he had already resigned himself to her death. He might simply accept it as a matter of course.

No. That seemed straightforward. It was what she would do if KD lived that bothered her.

Steffie had no apartment, and her job required her to

move around a lot. To constantly be in a different place at a different time. She had enough credits stored away that she could quit working altogether, but what was the point of that? Although she might have to, if she were responsible for KD.

At least Doctor Doom had guaranteed identification along with the successful surgery. That way, Steffie wouldn't have to brave the underground bureaucracy for her sister. All she had to concentrate on was teaching KD how to live in the real world.

It would fall to her. Her parents would never do the job. They might even try to keep the adult KD as imprisoned in their home as they had the child.

Steffie would have to warn KD of that.

Steffie brushed a strand of hair out of her face. She no longer felt clean from that shower she'd had at her parents' home. That was one disadvantage of flopping. She allowed herself to look as if she had been sleeping on the street more often than not.

And sometimes she did.

Maybe KD would help her settle down. Maybe KD would slow her down. It wouldn't hurt. She was, she had to admit, lonelier than she had expected in this life on the road.

Going back home had shown her that.

A man passed her wearing tight black leather pants with their ankles tucked inside cowboy boots, a muscle t-shirt and a derby. She had her palmtop open before she knew it and was recording. It didn't hurt to work. Not while she was waiting.

Not when Dr. Doom said it could take all day.

After she paid the dapper cowboy, she watched the street. It had been weeks since she'd been this far east in Manhattan. Fresh pickings of a kind she hadn't seen in a while. Fresh and bright. Something was changing here—an influx from somewhere, bringing, as they always did, new trends, new innovators, new ways to be original.

With Steffie around, they wouldn't be original for long.

She saw and rejected a woman with long green hair and a yellow rain slicker tied over her breasts, her tattooed stomach bare, and her hips barely covered in a matching yellow skirt. She hesitated over a man in the traditional garb of Scotland, complete with kilt. She had never seen such a thing outside of history shots. But it was too by-the-book, and that made it retro but unoriginal. Real retro took the style and updated it to the moment.

She had just finished catching her second big strike—a woman in white satin, a simple flowing dress that flared at the hips and crossed over her breasts. The back was cut all the way down to her buttocks, and in her hair she wore a matching white ribbon. The look was cool, casual, and completely unself-conscious—when Dr. Doom opened his door.

Actually, Dr. Doom didn't. His assistant did. He saw her flip a plastic at the satin woman, and looked away as if he had witnessed a drug deal.

"We're ready for you," he said.

[24]

THE LIGHTS WERE still bright in that sterile room, but the smell was different. The air was fresher as if each molecule had been personally scrubbed. A woman lay on the makeshift bed, a sheet pulled up to her chin. She was as tall as Steffie, and nearly as thin.

The assistant put his hand on her shoulder. "Don't be shocked," he said.

How could Steffie be shocked? The operation was successful. Her older sister looked older, for the first time since Steffie turned three.

Steffie walked up to KD and paused, her heart making a sudden lurch. This was what he was talking about. Not KD's size, but her face.

The skin was lumpy and mottled, broken as if it had tried to go through puberty in the space of a single afternoon. Which, she supposed, it had. KD's nose was truncated, her eyes suddenly small and piggy. Lines formed around her mouth, making it look sad and sour.

She was asleep.

Mercifully.

She didn't have to see Steffie's reaction.

"It's a side effect." The voice belonged to Dr. Doom. She hadn't seen him when she had come in, but he had been there, against the wall, gauging her reaction. "The problem is all her organs look like that. The damage is as obvious and as hard to repair."

"This is why the government shut you down," Steffie whispered.

"Yes," he said. "I can keep them alive, I can make them grow up, but I can't make them pretty. And people who do this to their kids expect pretty."

"How long does she have?" Steffie whispered.

"Years," he said. "And then, one day, something will shut down. But it was bound to happen. Her lifespan was truncated the moment she took those hormones."

Steffie was shaking. She sat on the bed, and took KD's hand. It was long and slender, the fingers curved inward, just like Steffie's. Only unlike Steffie's the skin on KD's hands was red and cracked, angry-looking, as if she'd kept them in hot water for days.

"She looks like this all over?" Steffie asked.

"Yes," he said.

Her mouth was dry. He was trying to extort more money from her.

It was working.

"Plastic surgery—"

"Isn't an option. The damage is cellular, and skin sloughs off, regrowing itself, regrowing the damage."

"But you work on the cellular level," Steffie said.

"And this is the best I've been able to do." His eyes were intense in his hangdog face. "I wouldn't leave her like this if I had a choice. Believe me."

"She's not going to be happy," Steffie said softly.

"She's alive," Dr. Doom said. "She's an adult. She'll be happy."

Steffie clutched her sister's hand tightly in her own. "I hope you're right," she said.

THE ASSISTANT GAVE her a blanket and a pillow, and rolled out a small cot for her. Steffie spent the night on it, her sleep shallow, any little noise waking her up. She kept expecting KD to return to consciousness, but she didn't. She had a lot to recover from, Doctor Doom explained, and she needed the rest.

He could have awakened KD at any point that night or the following day, but he did not. He let her sleep. He let her heal. Steffie had no choice but to sleep, and to brood.

She didn't want to leave KD's side, didn't want her sister—her frail older sister—to awaken alone and frightened. Steffie kept telling herself she would do this for anyone, but she knew the very thought was a lie.

She wouldn't do this for anyone.

She was surprising herself by doing it for KD. She didn't know if it was residual guilt, or if there was actually affection buried beneath all the anger, all the hurt, all the past.

When she did sleep, though, she dreamed of KD the little girl, when KD had truly been a little girl, and remembered all the times they laughed, all the days they huddled in each other's rooms, playing and enjoying each other's company.

Before Steffie got bigger. And KD didn't.

Now KD was big, but still flawed, and perhaps that was the other reason Steffie stayed. KD had hoped for a normal life.

And she would never have one.

On the morning of the second day, KD stirred. Steffie climbed off her cot and went to KD's side, suddenly conscious of the fact that she hadn't showered or changed clothes since she brought KD in.

KD's eyes fluttered, and a door opened beside her. Dr. Doom entered. He had probably been monitoring her from his private room.

KD's eyes opened. She looked at Dr. Doom, then at Steffie. "It worked?" she whispered. Her voice was a raspy croak but it was a deep raspy croak, the kind of woman's voice that made an alto sound as if she were singing first soprano. When KD realized it had come out of her, she giggled, a typical KD giggle, only deeper.

"I guess it did," she said, sitting up.

Dr. Doom was standing near Steffie. He put his hand on KD's shoulder. "There's a few things you should know," he said.

KD's gaze went from him to Steffie. Steffie did not smile, on purpose. KD frowned slightly.

"Look at your hands," Steffie said.

KD did. The frown grew deeper. She stroked the back

of the left with the long fingers of the right, then turned her left hand over as if it belonged to a stranger.

"The skin condition is permanent," Dr. Doom said. "And disfiguring. We can't do anything about it."

"How tall am I?" KD asked.

Dr. Doom took a deep breath, then smiled a little. The question shocked Steffie. "I don't know without you standing," he said. "I would guess about 5'7"."

"Five-seven," KD said. She raised her strange small eyes to Steffie. The eyes, even though they were small, still had KD in them. "I'm taller than you."

"Yes," Steffie said.

"I've never been taller than you."

"KD," Steffie said. "The skin—"

"Is disfiguring, yes, I know," KD said. "But it won't interfere with my life, will it?"

That last she addressed to Dr. Doom.

"People will stare at you. They will notice. They will not be kind."

KD shrugged. "That's my whole life," she said. "What else?"

"Your other organs are as damaged. You may not live a normal lifespan."

KD grinned. "I come back from the jaws of death an adult and you're worried about whether I'll live to ninety? I'm just glad I have tomorrow."

Steffie felt a strange tension in her shoulders. She had expected anger, screaming, tears, but she had never expected this calm acceptance, never figured that KD would take it all in stride.

"You knew," Steffie said. "You knew this was going to happen."

KD looked at her blankly, as if she couldn't understand the emotion that threaded through Steffie's voice. "I told you I read everything. And I had a long time to think about it. What would you rather have? Your freedom, your adulthood, or a pretty face? I had a pretty face for a long, long time. It didn't get me anywhere."

All that worry. All that agonizing. And KD was more prepared than Steffie gave her credit for. Steffie never really had trusted KD, never really had believed that there was an adult mind inside that child's body. KD played to everyone's prejudices so well.

"So, when can I go free?" KD asked Dr. Doom.

"As soon as we do a few tests," he said.

[26]

THE TESTS TOOK four hours. Steffie had to wait in a room she had not seen before while they were underway. When they were over, she went back into the room where she had slept and worried and stayed longer than any other place in New York.

The assistant had KD's new identification in a tray. Steffie looked it over, and realized that it not only looked authentic; it was authentic. The assistant had used KD's real birth records and put the factual information along with her vital statistics—height, weight, scars and distinguishing marks, and a hologram of her actual appearance. Adult identification, for a woman who had been on the Earth longer than Steffie had.

KD was sitting on the bed when Steffie entered, a series of chip monitors still attached to her left arm.

"We're nearly done," Dr. Doom said, and he sounded cheerful.

"Can we talk while you work?"

"Certainly," he said. "You should be happy to know she's turned out well. I expect great things of her."

KD smiled at him—the KD smile on that ravaged face.

"KD," Steffie said. "When we leave here, we need to deal with Mom and Dad. I could book you—"

"No," KD said. The smile left her face. It was suddenly blank. "I don't want to see them."

"But they'll want to know—"

"You tell them."

"All right," Steffie said, feeling out of her depth. KD was speaking with an anger foreign to Steffie. KD had always had anger, but not force behind it.

Not the force of a grown woman.

"We can decide that after we find a place," Steffie said. "I know a few apartments not far from here. They're large and not too expensive, and we'll each have our own entrances—"

"No," KD said again. Her small eyes narrowed. "You don't get it, Steffie. I'm done with all of you. I'm an adult now. I can do this on my own."

"I know," Steffie said. "But I thought—"

"You thought I'd need some protection in the big city. You thought I'd need to learn how to live. Well, I don't," KD said. She looked up at Dr. Doom. "We don't need her any more, do we?"

He glanced at Steffie. His expression was apologetic. "No," he said to KD. "You're an adult now. Legally. You can sign everything."

"Then that's it," KD said. "I'm sorry, Steffie. I know this was an inconvenience."

Steffie froze. What was KD doing? "Yeah," she said. "Yeah it was."

"Well, thanks," KD said. "I do appreciate it."

"That's obvious," Steffie snapped. Her initial feeling had been right. She had been manipulated.

Again.

KD had not been able to get anyone else to bring her to Dr. Doom.

She made Steffie.

She manipulated Steffie.

Masterfully.

KD pursed her lips. "There's no need to get upset. You've been moving on with your life a long time now. Just move past this one."

Steffie stared at her. It was an apt description. She had been moving, constantly moving, and mostly because of KD. And when she finally stopped, KD didn't want her. Didn't need her any more.

If she actually had needed Steffie, in the first place. Or if any adult would have done just as well.

"What do I tell Mom and Dad?" Steffie asked.

"Tell them I'm dead." KD was watching her out of that mockery of a face, the cracked and damaged skin twisting as she raised her eyebrows in typical KD you'd-better-believe-me fashion.

"I can't do that," Steffie said.

KD shrugged. "Then they'll always wonder."

"KD, you should go back there. Or call them. Or something. You owe them that much." Steffie couldn't believe she was arguing for her parents. She couldn't believe that

KD had put her in that position. She couldn't believe that anyone could put her in that position.

"Owe them?" KD's voice was unusually soft. Dr. Doom had stepped away from her slightly. The assistant was standing beside the door, holding Steffie's pouch. "I *owe* them? For what? Holding me prisoner all these years? Do you know what it's like, having an adult brain and not being allowed to use it? Do you know how many times I ran away, only to be returned to them like a lost puppy? Do you know how many times I begged to be let out of that house? No, Steffie. I don't owe them anything."

Steffie swallowed. She saw the hints around her, the signals from Dr. Doom and his assistant that she should leave.

She chose to ignore them.

"They loved you, in their own way."

"They loved a beautiful three-year-old doll they called KD because the name they had originally given her—before they decided to alter her—didn't suit a child." KD looked at her identification, then grinned at Dr. Doom.

"At least you got the name right," she said to him.

Steffie didn't have to look. She knew.

Kalianna Danita.

KD was right. The name was pretentious for a child, but it was suited to a woman, particularly a woman whose face had character and whose spirit matched.

"KD," Steffie said. "I've been on my own for a long time. At least let me help you start out."

"So that you can take the first opportunity to contact Mom and Dad?" KD shook her head. "Sorry, Steffie."

"KD," Steffie said, knowing she was losing this, but

having to try. "I won't contact them. It's just not easy out there. No matter what you think. No matter what you know."

KD's face went blank. "And you're an expert on this?"

"Actually, I am."

"Then maybe I will be too." She crossed her arms, and frowned. KD's frowns had been imposing as a child. They were twice as imposing on her adult face.

"You don't get it, Steffie," she said. "I don't want you around any more than I want Mom and Dad. I'm done with the family. I've done my time. I'm finished now."

"KD," Steffie said. "You're never done."

"You were," KD said.

"Until you brought me back."

"You thought I was dying."

Steffie shrugged. "You were. I helped."

"We're even." KD tilted her head back slightly. "Now get out."

"KD—"

"Get out."

Steffie stood there for a moment, unable to think. Unable to move. Then the assistant put his hand on her arm.

"Sorry," he said.

She glanced at KD, somehow thinking KD would change her mind, would be different.

But she wasn't even looking at Steffie.

It was as if Steffie were already gone.

Then the assistant tugged on Steffie's arm. She let him show her out.

At the main door, he stopped. "I'm sorry," he said

softly. "I've seen them do that before. I think it's part of the process. They've been objects so long, they don't realized when they're treating someone else the same way."

Steffie smiled at him, not really feeling any emotion behind the facial movement. Maybe he was right for other grown-up "children." Maybe. But for KD, it was merely her chance to act as the rest of the family had. To cut all ties, to make her own way.

Only her method had to be more drastic because her life had been so different.

"Do you contact the parents?" Steffie asked, knowing it was a cowardly question.

"No," he said.

She sighed. "I didn't think so," she said, and walked away.

[27]

SHE WALKED TO Central Park. It was, after all, the closest thing she had to a home in the city. She didn't cool-hunt on the way; she didn't even look at her surroundings. She could have been followed, she could have been mugged, but she didn't care.

She didn't quite understand what had happened to her, how she had suddenly lost her identity, had become KD's big little sister all over again.

Or maybe that identity never went away. Maybe she had buried it under years of running, years of hunting, years of flopping wherever time and the need took her.

She didn't like the way it had popped back up, the way it had opened her up to feelings like those she hadn't experienced since she was a girl.

Betrayal.

How could she feel betrayed by KD, when all KD had been trying to do was survive?

To have a life like Steffie did.

After all, KD was right.

Steffie had run out on her first.

And it had taken KD a long time to find her.

Was it revenge, then? Was that what KD had done? Or was it something less conscious, a simple action that had spiraled into something else?

Or maybe it was a combination of both, a simple action that became revenge. Because KD knew, perhaps better than Steffie did, that only a member of the family could have gotten her out of that house.

Steffie managed.

And now KD had her wish.

Steffie walked to her favorite bench and sat down. She had slept more in the last two days than she had slept in a long time, and yet she felt exhausted. Bone deep weary. So tired, she didn't want to hunt. So tired, she couldn't even decide what to do next.

A woman walked by wearing a pale peach tent shirt in a faux paisley pattern, brown gauze pants, and ribbon barrettes pulling her hair from her face. In her arms, she carried a small child wrapped in a blanket.

Steffie froze.

The woman wore boots just like the ones Steffie had on.

Only newer.

Steffie's ribbon barrettes were long gone, and her tent shirt was wrinkled beyond recognition. The brown pants were stained and ripped slightly from their odyssey the past two days.

Only Steffie knew the woman wore the same outfit Steffie did.

She sat still, holding her breath, scanning the park.

She saw a lot of people all going about their own business. None of them were looking at her.

Slowly she let her breath out, and as she did, she saw another young mother carrying a blanket wrapped child. Her ribbon barrettes did not match, nor did she have on the right boots.

Steffie resisted the urge to stand on her bench. She looked, more carefully this time, at the people on the paths, walking through the grass, sitting on the grass. Young couples, babies in carriers, bicyclists—

—and two more young women wearing her outfit, complete with child.

A male version walked past only moments later, the same except that he wore no ribbons in his short hair.

Not early adapters then. The style had been on the market long enough to be mass produced, long enough to be modified.

Someone had seen her the moment she got off the shuttle with KD, and had coolhunted her. And had shown no class, by not identifying himself, and by not paying her.

She was shaking. It wasn't the lack of money that bothered her. She had enough money. Nor was it even being coolhunted. It was bound to happen eventually. She had the right attitude, a focus on something else, with the clothes being secondary, but interesting.

No. None of those things disturbed her at all.

It was the lack of understanding.

She had been coolhunted at the most important moment of her life, and the marketing had gotten it all wrong, selling it to parents as a way of looking cool while carrying their child.

For her it had been a matter of life and death.

It had been the central moment of her adulthood. Everything crossed there—her childhood, her feelings about KD, and her future.

More than anything, her future.

She'd been willing to change it all for KD.

Steffie let out a small moan.

What was she going to do? Ignore it all and return to coolhunting, only to get it wrong like the person who had hunted her? How many people had she insulted, how many precious moments had she misunderstood? How much cool had simply been one of life's disasters proceeding in front of her, the trend-setter simply someone who had put on anything from his closet that day because he hadn't had time to think?

How many moments had she touched, and gotten wrong?

She stood, hand to her face. She couldn't go back to coolhunting. Coolhunting was the very thing that led to KD—to KD's imprisonment, to her life, to her rejection of everything she had known. What kind of person would KD have been if she had been allowed to develop normally?

Like Steffie.

"You all right, ma'am?" a woman asked. She was standing some distance away, as if she might catch something from Steffie if she got too close. But the woman had an expression on her face that implied that she had to ask, that she wouldn't have been able to live with herself if she hadn't.

No one had looked at her like that in a long, long time.

"I'm fine," Steffie said, doing her best to look normal, given her filthy clothing, her agitated state. "Really. Thank you."

The woman nodded, obviously not convinced, but not willing to argue. She continued down the path.

Steffie watched her go. What had the woman seen? A disheveled woman who lived on the streets? A woman who had just given her privacy to her sister, only to have the gift rejected?

Or a woman who looked lost, like Steffie felt?

For the first time in her life, she had nothing to run away from. Everything had run away from her.

Not even her mother pretended politeness any more. When they parted, her mother spoke words of love only to KD.

Steffie groaned again. Her mother expected news of KD, and KD certainly wasn't going to tell her.

Steffie couldn't just e-mail her. She couldn't just say that KD was dead.

And she couldn't ignore it and leave those two people alone together in that house. No matter what they'd done.

Or what she thought they'd done.

Maybe she had been wrong about them, too.

Maybe she hadn't understood their motives any better than she'd understood her own.

She put her hand back to her mouth, knowing her decision was made. She wasn't going to stay in Ann Arbor. She would take an afternoon shuttle there, and an evening shuttle back. And then she would get an apartment on Fifth Avenue with a view of the park.

And invest, maybe, or fashion gamble. She'd be good at that. Better than KD was.

And maybe playing online, she might even find KD.

Maybe.

But she doubted it.

To find someone, she had to be looking.

Her hunting days were over.

It was time to look beneath the surfaces to see what lurked in the depths.

And the first place she'd look was the last place anyone would expect her to look. Home.

To see what she had missed.

To see what the place was like without KD.

To take responsibility, for the first time, for her own actions.

She had rescued KD. She had brought change to that house.

Now she had to take it the last step.

Now she had to let her parents know that they could move forward, whether they wanted to or not.

She closed her eyes. Funny how she was always the one bringing change.

And she had finally brought it, to herself.

I value honest feedback, and would love to hear your opinion in a review, if you're so inclined, on your favorite book retailer's site.

Be the first to know!

Just sign up for the Kristine Kathryn Rusch newsletter, and keep up with the latest news, releases and so much more— even the occasional giveaway.

So, what are you waiting for? To sign up go to kristinekathrynrusch.com.

But wait! There's more. Sign up for the WMG Publishing newsletter, too, and get the latest news and releases from all of the WMG authors and lines, including Kristine Grayson, Kris Nelscott, Dean Wesley Smith, *Fiction River: An Original Anthology Magazine, Smith's Monthly,* and so much more.

To sign up go to wmgpublishing.com.

New York Times bestselling author Kristine Kathryn Rusch writes in almost every genre. Generally, she uses her real name (Rusch) for most of her writing. Under that name, she publishes bestselling science fiction and fantasy, award-winning mysteries, acclaimed mainstream fiction, controversial nonfiction, and the occasional romance. Her novels have made bestseller lists around the world and her short fiction has appeared in eighteen best of the year collections. She has won more than twenty-five awards for her fiction, including the Hugo, *Le Prix Imaginales*, the *Asimov's* Readers Choice award, and the *Ellery Queen Mystery Magazine* Readers Choice Award.

Publications from *The Chicago Tribune* to *Booklist* have included her Kris Nelscott mystery novels in their top-ten-best mystery novels of the year. The Nelscott books have received nominations for almost every award in the mystery field, including the best novel Edgar Award, and the Shamus Award.

She writes goofy romance novels as award-winner Kristine Grayson.

She also edits. Beginning with work at the innovative publishing company, Pulphouse, followed by her award-winning tenure at *The Magazine of Fantasy & Science Fiction*, she took fifteen years off before returning to editing with the original anthology series *Fiction River,* published by WMG Publishing. She acts as series editor with her husband, writer Dean Wesley Smith, and edits at least two anthologies in the series per year on her own.

To keep up with everything she does, go to kriswrites.com and sign up for her newsletter. To track her many pen names and series, see their individual websites (krisnelscott.com, kristinegrayson.com, retrievalartist.com, divingintothewreck.com).

kriswrites.com

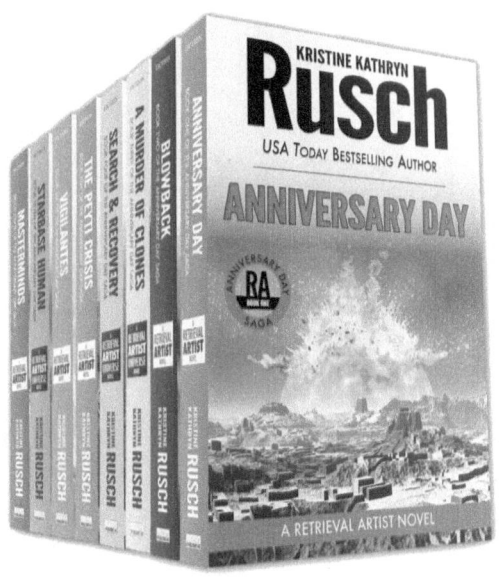

THE ANNIVERSARY DAY SAGA

Eight novels.
One explosive storyline.

"Anniversary Day is an edge-of-the-seat thriller that will keep you turning pages late into the night and it's also really good science fi tion. What's not to like?."
—*Analog*

Available at your favorite bookseller.